The Savannah Stories

With This Ring

The Savannah Stories

With This Ring

J.L. Lemon

ISBN-13: 978-0-9909589-0-1

Published 2015

Original title: Walking On Broken Glass

Printed by Lulu.com in the United States of America

This book is dedicated to my family – each and every one that has believed in me. I am thankful for you all.

This book is also dedicated to my family who now dine at God's supper table. They've got the best view and the best Team Captain.

Faith is like electricity.

You can't see it, but you can see the light.

- Author Unknown

1

"George and Martha Washington," Ennis began.

"Ginger Rogers and her five ex-husbands," Savannah volleyed back.

"Rosa and Raymond Parks. Nearly forty-five years."

"Zsa Zsa Gabor and Felipe De Alba. Nearly twenty-four hours."

Ennis sighed. Savannah knew she was winning again – and so did he. The mention of marriage summoned a debate over success or failure every time. She loved Ennis with all her heart but marriage presented a portent of hell for her, at least in her own mind. For basically a year and a half, she and Ennis shared their lives as partners on the Atlanta Police Department. Spending days (and plenty of nights) together on the job, the two detectives naturally grew closer until six months ago when they promoted their relationship to lovers as well. It didn't matter to her that he was younger by three years at an energetic, well muscled twenty-seven. The age difference also neglected to dampen his enthusiasm. In truth, it inspired him to romance her and attempt to sway her to his way of thinking. One thing about Ennis Rutherford: his passion for her far outweighed his common sense. That's why marriage talk inevitably ended in a tug of war that she always won.

Savannah knew if they ever wedded, their partner days were over. The department split married cops into two different locations. She didn't want her or especially Ennis assigned to a bad part of town.

To her, life was good single. With Ennis basically living with her, they enjoyed all the perks of matrimony without the threat of divorce. What she feared most – Ennis eventually falling out of love with her. She was difficult to live with, she realized that so when she thought too long or hard about accepting his proposal, the vision of Ennis walking out the door stopped her cold. Marriage invited trouble, starting with discontent and ending in divorce. Bottom line, she couldn't bear to lose Ennis – in any respect.

Behind the wheel of his Dodge Ram, Ennis contemplated her response then accused, "You made that up. Zsa Zsa and who?"

A smile crossed her face, "See? Shortest marriage in history."

"Okay, how about Ronald and Nancy Reagan?"

"Ennis, find someone other than presidents who stayed married. It's a no-brainer. Presidents stay married because it's good for their image." He'd begun this curious banter as they pulled away from the police station to go home. Since progress was slow on their current case, they decided to call it a day, grab a burger and go home. They weren't but five blocks from their favorite restaurant when Ennis blurted, "Morticia and Gomez Addams. As Gomez said 'I would die for her. I would kill for her. Either way, what bliss.'"

Savannah's expression questioned his sanity, "Number one, don't joke about dying. Number two, I thought we were staying with real people. I'm revoking your next choice of June and Ward Cleaver so here's my response. Romeo and Juliet."

Her partner let out a belly laugh. Amused, Savannah watched Ennis double in the seat. Had it been anyone else, she'd have flown mad, but this was her darling Ennis, title-holder to "sexiest male in existence". Whether talking, laughing or murmuring sweet nothings in her ear, she loved hearing his deep tone roll like soft thunder.

After several seconds, he regained his composure but

only barely, "You're slipping *and* changing the rules. Romeo and Juliet weren't even married."

"They were planning on it, though."

"The rules were people who were actually hitched. So," he drew an imaginary line in the air, "chalk one up for me. I'm gaining on you."

"Have it your way but I have the crown jewel on my side. Staying with your fictional couples who were married, I choose Rhett and Scarlett. They split up, if you remember the story correctly."

"You'll start an avalanche you're losing ground so fast. Scarlett was in love with another man, you're not." He then amended, "I hope."

Savannah slanted him a look of disbelief, "Did you fall and hit your head? After dinner, I'll show you precisely where you stand with me, sonny."

They drove silently for another block when she noticed he glimpsed at her from the corner of his eye. Suddenly he braked and spun the steering wheel into a tight turn, causing her to grab the dashboard for stability. "What are you doing?" she asked.

A wily grin crept across his cheeks, "I always had to eat my dinner before I had dessert. Tonight, no one's stopping me from indulging in a heaping helping of sweet Savannah." He bobbed his brow at her, "Then we'll talk about dinner."

O   O   O

Ennis typically drove like a madman but when aroused, he redefined the definition of crazy. The Dodge Ram's diesel engine rumbled lazily at stop lights only to roar when Ennis bore down on the accelerator. Savannah knew to watch traffic while he busied himself shifting gears and checking the road ahead. "Ennis," she said in a reasonably calm voice, "the bed'll still be there, whether we're two minutes earlier or not."

He grimaced at the reference to the bed, "You try driving rationally with a boner."

The declaration brought a smile as she looked away. Ennis always had an answer. As it turned out, they arrived home in record time, considering the evening traffic still snarled in places. The Dodge squealed to a stop in her driveway and before she knew it, she and Ennis were racing for the door. Ennis caught her from behind, his arms slipping around her waist to hold her close. He pressed a slow, warm kiss to the back of her neck.

"I can't think straight when you do that," she sighed.

He chuckled, the sound creating a tickle on her sensitive skin, "That's what I'm counting on, sugar."

Savannah forced herself to focus and slide the key in the lock. One solid twist on the knob opened the way for them. Ennis guided her over the threshold, his hold still snug around her. He turned her in his arms and using one hand, closed the door behind her. Ennis urged her against the wooden door while freeing her hair from the ponytail.

"You're wicked, Detective Rutherford," she teased. "You're the man my mama warned me about."

A devilish grin appeared, "And you didn't listen, you foolish girl." His fingers threaded her hair to cup the back of her head as his lips descended to hers.

Savannah met him halfway, a soft moan punctuating the instant they met. She wound her arms around his neck to hold him to the steamy kiss – though truth was neither planned to come up for air anytime soon. His mouth hungrily covered hers, deepening the kiss, and Savannah trembled at the rasp of his day old beard. The sensation brought memories of Ennis using the roughness in decidedly more sensitive places. Along with clever, she'd label her partner as roguishly sensual when he put his mind to it.

Ennis tightened his embrace when their tongues met. He

pressed into her, the heat and strength of his body against hers sent a quiver of desire through her. When he said he wanted dessert he meant it, judging by the arousal nestled at her belly.

The urgency of the kiss ebbed into a slow, savoring pleasure. They took their time exploring, Ennis especially, since she felt his hands glide down her sides, his thumbs brushing lightly across both nipples. Savannah's breath caught and Ennis smiled against her lips.

His hands traveled down until she felt him plucking her .38, holster and all, from her belt. He sat it on the entry table and followed it with her handcuffs, cell phone and badge. Finally, Ennis flattened his palm against her back, holding her close. He eased away from the kiss though his lips lingered close, "Fair warning. I'm planning to take full advantage of you."

Savannah struggled to formulate a coherent thought, "I would consider that coercion on your part."

He smiled easily at that, teasing, "I can find exciting ways to coerce you, you know."

She returned the smile with a gentle nudge against his crotch, "Then by all means, coerce away."

Ennis dipped just enough to sweep her, weightless, into his arms. Savannah leaned in for another kiss while he made his way to the bedroom.

O O O

Savannah watched Ennis sleep. She dared not move for fear of waking him. He squeezed her close after their lovemaking, as if any separation from her was unbearable. In truth, she felt the same way. She still lay with her head on his broad, hairy chest, and one leg drawn over his thighs. His hand remained crooked under her knee, holding her leg in the position. He'd spent countless minutes tracing the line of her back until gifting her with a contented smile and sliding his hand over the curve of her bottom. His long fingers splayed out on her skin, squeezed her tenderly then gently drew her leg across his. Savannah snuggled into his embrace while his touch glided along the back of her thigh until settling at her knee. Before Ennis, she never allowed herself to relax in a man's arms. He made trusting him easy and most of all, he made loving him easy.

In the carpet of dark chest hair was her hand, following the gentle rise and fall of his breathing. She never felt so safe in an embrace, so loved. Ennis cherished her in and out of bed and she attempted to do the same for him. Growing up, love and support died with her mother, leaving her with an abusive father whose idea of closeness only applied to Johnnie Walker scotch. Savannah admitted emotional intimacy was her short suit. Most of her relationships ended before physical intimacy entered the picture. Of those men, none came close to Ennis Rutherford. Her partner resided in an entirely different universe. Ennis took time to break down barriers to acquaint himself with her. He tolerated her temper and quirks, overlooked them and dug deeper until finally she surrendered and opened up.

When she did, he treaded lightly on sensitive subjects. He allowed time for her to elaborate further – if she chose not to, he dropped it. Men weren't like this, her mind initially warned. Men were pushy for answers. If they were refused, they resorted to abuse, either physical or emotional. Men were cruel creatures who thrived on tearing down their mates.

She struggled with that logic for months, convinced that Ennis would ultimately hurt her or break her heart. Trust never came easy for her. Trust with men never happened, not until Ennis.

Savannah pressed a soft kiss to his chest. He stirred slightly, his hold barely tightened around her back but he stayed asleep. She hadn't imagined loving the feel of a man like she did Ennis. They'd been together long enough she memorized him from head to toe. She was damn sure he'd memorized her, especially all her ticklish spots and sensual ones. Even his smell drove her wild. Most times he'd forego the cologne, leaving the subtle scent of soap and one hundred percent male.

She felt the beginnings of a smile inch across her lips. Maybe she was nuts. Perhaps she'd been alone too long but she knew one thing without a doubt. She loved Ennis Rutherford with all her heart.

Her vision wandered to her left hand lifting and falling with his breathing. Lately she toyed with the idea of marriage, though she'd never tell Ennis. One sign of her cracking and he'd drag her to the preacher, either by her hand or by her feet. She'd never seen a man so anxious to get hitched. That was unnatural in itself. Men tended to pull away from commitment, not women. The fact she declined to commit and he refused to give up told her a lot. He either suffered a hit on the head somewhere along the way or he really loved her. She believed the latter considering he regularly declared his love for her. The last few months, she found returning the sentiment not only easier but essential. She wanted him to realize how much he meant to her. Mrs. Ennis Rutherford. She played the name around in her head a moment. The smile broadened and she appraised her left hand again, deciding a ring really wouldn't look bad at all.

2

Exactly one week after their marriage debate in the car,
Savannah found herself buried in paperwork. For two hours
she'd been cooped up in her small office typing out reports for
the current case while Ennis sidetracked to shop. Instinctively,
she kept peeking at the calendar. Today was hers and Ennis's
anniversary. Although they weren't married, he insisted on
keeping track of their monthly anniversaries with little gifts and
romantic evenings together. This month marked their
eighteenth month as professional partners, their fourteenth as
romantic partners. She'd picked up a gift for him – a new
watch. A Rolex it wasn't but it had enough bells and whistles to
keep Ennis smiling for quite a while. Plus, it used sunlight and
artificial light to recharge the battery. She *knew* he'd enjoy that.
The idea of a watch sounded strange to her sister Georgia when
she'd mentioned it. Savannah lifted a brow and shrugged,

"He's been saying he wants another watch. So I bought him one and had it engraved on the back."

Georgia asked what the engraving said. When Savannah blushed, her sister backed off knowingly, "Nevermind. It's obviously too personal to share."

Savannah and Ennis made plans to exchange their gifts and celebrate that night. Their celebrations normally left her boneless with pleasure and him snoring like a freight train. She looked forward to this evening more than ever, seemed like. That's why, when a nagging nausea crept into her gut, she winced, hoping it passed quickly. She worked a while longer with expectations that the feeling might diminish. Instead, it reinforced itself and gave her pause about eating anymore Rocketburgers with jalapeño peppers.

It grew so intense she grabbed four Tums and still entertained a pint of milk from the coffee room. A sudden commotion only deepened the sickness. A yell broke the usual hum of voices, quieting the entire station house. A man's voice called out again, this time inserting her name, "Is Prince in her office?"

Detective John Mathis strolled by with a frown – no doubt he planned to call down the young cop for his brash behavior. There were times when new cops let their enthusiasm override better judgment and the veteran cops felt it their sworn duty to admonish them. "This ain't no zoo," she'd heard Mathis once say. "And we don't need no hearing aids so stifle it." This time, however, the heavyset Mathis stopped upon sight of the rookie then glanced in to see the confusion on her face. He answered back, "Yeah, why?"

"I'm taking her to Atlanta Medical."

Mathis crooked his finger at her, concern furrowing his brow. Nothing shook John Mathis but something in his expression produced a tidal wave of alarm inside her. Savannah's mind cleared like clouds parting the sky. By this time she was on her feet and at the door to see a uniform officer hesitantly approaching her. The kid barely looked twenty and she knew he'd finished training with his Field Training Officer no more than two weeks earlier. The expression on his face reminded her of a deer in the headlights. He swallowed hard when his wide eyes connected to hers, and the blood drained from his narrow face.

Savannah recognized his look. She'd encountered it plenty of times as a rookie and it almost always involved a rookie's "first". The first sight of a gunshot wound, rolling up on their first bad car accident, the sight of their first dead body, and her all time worst experiences: seeing her first dead child, and the helplessness of someone dying while she tried to save them.

Her vision lowered to his hands. Cradled in them were a cell phone, a holstered .38 and a gold shield on top. Her heart jumped in her throat, her own hands began trembling. When she focused on the badge number, she instantly felt sicker than she had in several years. Mathis bent closer to survey the contents of the rookie's hands. A second later Savannah felt John gently squeeze her shoulder as she forced herself to ask the question she dreaded the answer to, "What happened to Ennis?"

The officer's vision shifted downward, "Detective, you need to come with me." He reached out, offering the badge, weapon and phone to her. He held them gingerly yet it seemed he couldn't relinquish custody of them fast enough.

Mathis watched her accept them, and stared as her thumb stroked the badge. He turned his attention to the young officer. John possessed little patience, especially with rookies. He assumed the responsibility of teaching them protocol as he deemed necessary. Today he deemed it crucial, "C'mon, answer her. Is Rutherford okay?"

The look on – Savannah glanced at his nametag – Meade's face said it all. What she required was the reassurance that Ennis was, at least, alive. The sickness plaguing her intensified as Meade stalled to find the right words. She could have told him the search was always futile. Just tell the person who, what and how. Panic mixed with temper as she blurted, "Tell me he's okay."

Meade glanced from beneath his bowed head. Evidently he finally realized he wasn't just in the spotlight, he was the whole show, "He's been shot," he mumbled self-consciously. "Please come with me. I'll tell you in the car."

She raced back to her office for her purse and jacket. In less than three minutes she sat in the front seat of a cruiser, the siren blaring. Savannah fought the nausea making a return trip, only it grew worse. Any other day she'd blame it on the wild driving. The thought reminded her of how Ennis flew around corners in his Acura. She was never so happy to see him trade vehicles, even for the huge Dodge Ram that dwarfed her driveway. She swallowed back the sickness, and uttered an expletive that described only a modicum of her annoyance, "At least tell me he's not dead."

Meade concentrated on watching traffic while driving. The dark haired rookie looked left, right, ahead of them and in the rearview mirror. He purposely avoided eye contact with her which both terrified and angered her. The kid had plenty to learn about law enforcement – if he subsequently survived her wrath. Informing loved ones of a tragedy rated about nil on a cop's joy scale anyway. Prolonging the agony fueled scores of negative emotions, all directed at the reluctant cop. She was no different. If Meade didn't start talking soon, she'd start breaking things, beginning with his head.

The cruiser bucked and bounced through intersections, sending her stomach into her throat. "When I left him," Meade finally responded, "he was still alive." He quickly scanned the intersection then punched the accelerator.

She released a sigh of relief with the urge to cry bubbling close to the surface. The front of the car dipped, however, telling her to brace for the rebound. She hadn't been that sick since her first partner, Riley Murphy, sat at the wheel. At the rate Meade drove, she'd be lucky not to reside at Atlanta Medical herself.

He completed a turn so violently she swore she was at Six Flags. His foot pushed the gas again, "He was shot trying to stop a rape. The perp got away but a witness called the police. When I rolled on scene, Detective Rutherford kept asking for you. I waited for the ambulance then came for you."

The words fought to remain unspoken. Her heart raced a million miles an hour and it panged with every beat. Ennis was hurt and asking for her. From the instant she realized he was in trouble, her eyes threatened to cry a river. Some of the tears began streaking her face. She didn't want to ask the next question. Her heart implored her not to but her brain won the battle, "Where was he shot?"

Meade still refused to look at her. *That's a bad sign,* her mind warned. Instead, he kept his vision straight ahead while weaving in and out of traffic. He took a deep breath, "In the chest."

With that declaration, the car sped violently around a corner, forcing her to cling to the dashboard. In the last ten minutes her life went from perfect to perfect shit. Unlike patrol officers, detectives weren't required to wear protective vests on the job unless the situation warranted it. Excluding Christmas, shopping wasn't exactly hazardous. A thousand questions poised on her tongue all at once. "Where in the chest?" she wanted to ask, as well as, "Was the shot at close range?" So many questions mounted that her mind jumbled every question into a useless soup of words.

Meade swung a glimpse past her, "It happened near the florist shop closest to Phipps Plaza." The cop managed to maneuver the cruiser at a decent rate of speed while reaching beside him in the seat, "He also wanted me to give you this."

Savannah existed in a surreal world now. She'd had plenty of nightmares however those paled in comparison to the truth. Ennis may die without hearing her biggest surprise of all. She wanted to wait until their anniversary – and his customary reference to marriage – to finally say yes to him.

The cop held out a long, flat, beautifully wrapped box. It was pink with a white ribbon that read "Tiffany & Co." It looked like the size of a necklace box. Swallowing hard, she purposefully tucked it in her purse, "He can give it to me later. Thank you."

Magically she found herself at the Atlanta Medical emergency entrance. The cop bounded out his door and opened hers before she even touched the handle. "My prayers are with you and Detective Rutherford, ma'am. If you need anything, let me know."

She nodded an acknowledgment with the assumption he escorted her inside. Truthfully, she only focused on the location of the nurse's kiosk. Everything else blurred into irrelevance. Savannah ran straight to the admittance desk, "Ennis Rutherford. Where is he?"

The nurse went to work thumbing folders, searching. Images of Ennis lying in the emergency room calling for her spurred Savannah to present her shield and basically plead,

"I'm his partner so *please* hurry."

The nurse glanced up at her and saw the panic in her features.   She finally settled on one folder, studied it momentarily then informed, "He's in room four but –"

Savannah took off running in the direction the nurse pointed. She had to get to Ennis. She had to let him know she was there for him – and that she always would be.

She raced down the crowded hallway, slipping between doctors and nurses while counting off emergency room numbers.   Suddenly she applied her brakes and practically skidded past his room and into another person when she laid eyes on her partner through the window.   The once strong, genial man laid stone still on the gurney as nurses and doctors surrounded him.   Everything seemed to move in slow motion. She heard the muffled voices inside the room, none of them belonging to Ennis.   The scope of her vision tapered to encompass only her beloved to focus on him. She heard herself call his name even as her body rebelled at the sight of his motionless form.   She felt faint and her knees threatened to buckle. Trying to steady herself, she braced her hands on the glass window.

Savannah told herself to straighten up and not cry but this situation blindsided her, much like when her mother was admitted to the hospital. She squeezed her eyes shut tight, purging memories of that time. It wouldn't happen twice. The necessity of the emergency room was a fluke. The fact she was, for a second time, called away from her job with bad news was coincidence as well. She stared at Ennis through the window – she remembered doing the same thing with Charlene – and instantly jumped back a step like the window was on fire. *No, she gritted her teeth, not again...* Ennis would live, she tried to tell herself. Unlike her mother, he'd leave the hospital good as new. Ennis would live. Ennis had to live.

"Peach," a voice softly called from beside her. When she turned, a man looking amazingly similar to Ennis opened his arms wide then smothered her in a big bear hug. The tears came easily and freely while in Dane's arms. Despite being the same age as she, Savannah considered Ennis's brother more an older brother to her. They'd grown close over the past several months – closer than even she and Seth were as siblings – so when his arms closed around her, she melted into his embrace.

A touch on her shoulder brought her tearful vision to her sister. She knew panic mixed with confusion registered with Georgia who explained, "The officer used Ennis's cell phone to call me. He said he'd pick you up and bring you." Her expression sobered to the point Savannah feared she'd say the worst. She couldn't cope with one certain phrase. Many years earlier, Georgia broke the news their mother had passed away. Back then, she'd used two simple words to destroy Savannah, "She's gone." Remembering those words now, she backpedaled from Dane's embrace, the threat in her voice plain as day, "Don't say he's gone. Don't you dare say it, Georgia."

Her sister changed from dire to dumbfounded in two seconds. Then, like the same memory emerged from long ago, her expression softened, "Honey, he's not gone but he's hurt pretty bad. The doctor thinks –"

The mere mention threw Savannah into a fit of crying that her sister attempted to calm, "The doctor thinks he'll be okay if they can get the bullet out. Savannah," she called, trying to obtain her line of vision. "*Listen to me.* The doctor believes Ennis will be okay if they can remove the bullet."

She worked to dry her tears – a feat that became monumental since her mind continually flashed images of the brawny, handsome man she loved beyond any description, even beyond human reason. Sweet, gentle Ennis. The only man she'd truly trusted, that she truly loved, "I'm such a mess. I have to gather myself before I see him."

"Peach, they won't let you in there," Dane said.

"Yes, they will," she declared with steel determination.

She handed her purse to him and raced inside, wiping tears as she went. She willed herself to stop crying, to show Ennis the strength he'd shown her numerous times. He needed her calm and supportive, not weepy and falling apart.

The doctor saw her first, "Ma'am, you'll have to leave. We're prepping him for surgery –"

She flashed her badge and rounded the side of the gurney, "He's my partner and fiancé." She looked down and the dizziness returned full force. They stripped him of clothes, leaving only a sheet covering him to the waist. Various monitors were placed on his chest, and at least two IVs ran fluids into his arm. But what consumed her vision was the wound in the left side of his chest, a few inches below his shoulder. She instinctively reached to touch him, her fingers stopping short of the wound and settled at the line of hair above his navel. His skin was warm and moist, not unlike the feel of his skin after they made love. She took a deep breath, trying to bolster her courage to speak calmly to him.

They'd cleaned around the wound and shaved that portion of his chest, highlighting the bullet hole in a wide halo of white skin. He looked so still it scared her. His face was pale, his eyes closed. It reminded her of the many people she'd seen on a concrete slab in the morgue. Driving out the macabre images, she lifted her vision to his handsome face. She touched his cheek, feeling the light rasp of his beard, "Ennis, baby, it's me. I'm here." She bent down and kissed his forehead, "I'm finally here."

He didn't move which rooted the panic deeper. She called him again, this time with more determination in her voice. He would open his eyes if she had to scream to do it. She wanted proof Ennis still lived, proof she hadn't lost her best friend.

His eyelids slowly and lazily opened to narrowly reveal his handsome dark eyes. His lips moved in a weak fashion and instead of hearing her name, she read it from his lips.

He looked so vulnerable it brought more tears to her eyes, "You're gonna be all right, baby, just hang in there."

"I love you," his hoarse voice declared, his trembling hand moving to hers.

She wrapped her hand around his, holding on and never wanting to let go. Her other cradled his cheek and she kissed him gently on the lips, "I love you too. I'm here for you now and always. Once you're back on your feet, we need to discuss a wedding."

The words opened his eyes slightly more. She was thankful he was still conscious enough the statement registered.

His hold tightened on her hand, "You'll marry me?"

She pressed a kiss to his knuckles then held his hand to her cheek, remembering and savoring the feel, "I will, Ennis. The first opportunity we have, we're getting married."

A tiny smile curved his lips and he whispered, "I finally broke you."

Savannah couldn't contain a teary laugh as she intertwined their fingers, "Thoroughly and completely. I want to be your wife, Ennis, and I wouldn't have anyone else as my husband."

She never realized how much marriage meant to her, at least with Ennis. The pain she suffered just knowing he was in trouble – the physical and emotional pain – was excruciating. She couldn't lose him. And if they both retired from the job and raised chickens and ducks for a living, it was damn fine with her as long as they were together.

"Detective, we really need to get him into surgery," the doctor urged softly.

The gurney began moving as they wheeled him into the hallway. Dane and Georgia stepped aside to let them pass. Savannah followed alongside Ennis, her hand still holding his, her lips kissing his knuckles, "I'll be waiting for you, baby."

He swallowed dryly and cringed as he drew a shallow

breath. Just before passing through the surgery doors, his voice sounded as faint as his squeeze on her hand, "I'll be back, Mrs. Rutherford."

o   o   o

Shortly after Ennis left for surgery, Savannah disappeared and her absence worried both Georgia and Dane. They split forces to find her with Georgia heading outside and Dane searching indoors.

He covered so many square feet of area, he swore he'd walked to Alabama and back. He hadn't pegged her for a flight risk considering how close she and Ennis were. Georgia maintained her sister wouldn't go far but after a solid twenty minutes of intense hunting, Dane wasn't so sure.

He left the cafeteria for the gift shop. By then he stumbled on an out of the way door. The small sign to the side read "Chapel". Needing a breather, he decided to stop, rest, and while he was there, send up a few prayers for his brother.

When Dane opened the chapel doors, he heard the sounds of quiet weeping. The place appeared empty except for the noise. He slowly walked toward the sound, searching the pews until finally finding Savannah kneeling in front of a twelve foot statue of Jesus, his arms outstretched and welcoming. Her hands covered her face as mournful sobs racked her. The sound reminded him of his mother's weeping when his father passed. Dane purged his mind of the painful memories and focused on the sight before him. While heartbreaking, the image also confused him since Ennis told him Savannah didn't believe in God. But, as Dane knew, personal crisis and tragedy drew lost souls to His love for comfort. She certainly wouldn't be the first or last. The scene both warmed his heart and broke it. She looked like a scared child searching for a familiar, friendly face.

Dane kneeled at her side and brought her into his embrace, "Peach, you don't have to bear this alone. Georgia and I are here for you."

"I know," she wept, "but everyone's concerned about him. They don't need me adding to their worries."

Dane tightened his hold, "We care about you too. We all know how nuts you are about Ennis." That was no understatement either. He'd never seen two people so crazy over each other that *weren't* hitched.

"He was trying to stop a rape." She sucked in a trembling breath, "Ennis is so gentle, so thoughtful." Lifting her vision to Dane's, she blinked tears from her reddened eyes then crumbled again, "I love him so much."

Dane pressed her close again, "And he loves you. My brother is pretty darned bullheaded. That boy will fight anyone and anything to stay with you."

"I should have been with him. I could have protected him. I let him down."

And there was the guilt she shouldered. Dane waited for the confession to eventually come to light. She felt responsible for not being there, for not protecting Ennis.

"Savannah, this isn't your fault. If you were there the guy could have easily shot you too. You didn't let Ennis down. Plus, you heard Georgia. The doctor believes he'll be okay if they can get the bullet out."

"If *this*, if *that*..." she paused then hesitated as though contemplating his words. "Wait. Why would they have trouble removing it?"

Big mouth, Dane chided himself. He managed, as every male Rutherford did, to stick his foot in his mouth without even salting it first. Their daddy always said, "If you find yourself in a hole, the first thing to do is stop digging." Dane never learned to perfect that trick. In fact, all the boys had a talent for digging holes. Dane not only dug them but now he'd resorted to pushing himself in too. Searching for the right words became futile. He should tell her the truth but considering her current state of mind, he settled for, "Honey, they always say stuff like that."

Savannah looked him directly in the eyes and he sensed her measuring his expression, words and posture. Her features registered the distinctive fact she detected a fib. Dane fought the urge to shrink back and slink to the waiting room.

Savannah blinked once, wiped a tear or two then shook her head, "No, they don't. What aren't you telling me?"

"What makes you think I'm holding back?"

"I can see it in your eyes. Dane, tell me."

He tried to retain a solid front as she stared at him. The tears trembling on her eyelids broke him over, "Aw, hell. They said he'd lost a lot of blood and that getting the bullet might create complications. That's not to say he's gonna die, Peach. Don't think that." The fear in her red-rimmed blue eyes told him that's exactly what she thought. Faith hadn't been an active player in her life for many years, according to Ennis. He'd warned Dane not to preach God, prayer or religion to her unless he just enjoyed licking his wounds. Since he already hemorrhaged from basically chewing on his foot, he carefully treaded into the matter, "Do you pray often?"

Savannah instantly retreated emotionally and physically.

She backed away, her arms wrapped around her knees, the tears faded. The drastic change amazed him. One mention of prayer and she hardened to stone. She sniffed, wiped her face with one swipe of her palm and shook her head, "Praying never worked for me. When I was younger I tried but Daddy kept beating us. I tried again when my mama was sick. She died with me praying she wouldn't. God doesn't listen to me."

He ducked his head to see her features. She was steadfast about the subject. Despite that, he couldn't ignore the irony, "If you don't mind me asking, why are you in the chapel if God doesn't listen?"

"It was just a place to go, to get away from the noise."

Dane sat back, resting against the pew. "Peaceful in here, isn't it?"

She momentarily debated her answer, settled for, "It's quiet, yes."

He contemplated how to proceed. One option, to shut up, didn't set well with him. He chose the other alternative, to plod on knowing she'd probably get pissed. "Y'know, our daddy had a talent for dispensing wisdom. He grew up the son of a cattle rancher and those folks develop a unique insight to life. They have to since they have their fair share of trouble and heartache." Dane noticed she finally settled into a receptive mood so he continued, "He told us boys, 'When you're heading down a long road with a heavy load, don't look back and don't look too far ahead. Just keep taking it a step at a time and you'll get there.' Ennis ever said that?"

The corners of her mouth lifted a degree, "More or less."

"From what Georgia has said, your ma sounds a lot like our daddy. Giving advice in her own way. She also said your ma was a spiritual woman."

"Dane, please don't –"

"Just hear me out, Peach," he gently urged. "Don't you think your ma would want you to give prayer one more try?"

"Probably, but God and I aren't on speaking terms at the current time."

The anger in her voice caused him to back down somewhat, "That's too bad." He waited a minute before pointing to the statue of Jesus, "That image comforts me."

She didn't reply but cut her vision to the statue then back to him. The set of her mouth telegraphed how disgruntled she felt at the mention of anything remotely religious. He needed to tread lightly now, "It gives me hope, Savannah, and it reminds me that God is with me and hears me. I've been praying a lot today and I can feel the Lord comfort me."

"Good for you," she answered. The longer she sat and

mulled over his statement, the more bitter her words became, "You must have more influence upstairs than I do."

"Nope, I don't think so. I believe He's with you too. I believe that's why you retreated to the chapel. God wants you to talk to Him."

"No," she sneered, "He really doesn't."

"Let's give it a try, shall we?" Dane moved to his knees and drew her closer again. Initially she resisted his effort until he added, "Let's do it for Ennis. We'll both sit here and pray and see if God hears you."

3

Savannah, Georgia, and Dane sat together in the waiting room. Numerous conversations hummed steadily through the room. Tinny applause rattled from a small TV in the corner. The excess noise grated on her but she managed to contain her temper. Expending any energy past helping Ennis was definitely not in the neighborhood of smart, especially when a rabble of kids huddled around the TV and their mothers looked grateful for a break. Savannah opted to take a breath instead of disturbing the room's emotional balance.

Instead, she tried to busy herself sizing up the renovated waiting room. The walls went from stark white to a warmer taupe with matching couches and chairs. The color provided more comfort unlike the actual furniture. Savannah likened it to surplus from the Inquisition. The chair's padding provided enough comfort for perhaps thirty minutes then aches began to appear. Her back hurt, her neck was stiff and her knees began singing a loathsome song that demanded pain relief.

The second hour of Ennis's surgery ticked by uneventfully except Seth arrived to join the group. Savannah's oldest sibling inevitably acted like an outcast until sizing up the situation. She assumed being an ex-army Ranger made him more cautious than normal. Having an overtly candid personality also contributed to his cautious demeanor. Seth could piss off the Pope, she was convinced of it. Even Georgia nursed a long running rift with Seth so, months earlier, when her brother declared Savannah "just like Pops" because of her temper, she hoped he detected a chill in the air when around her. At least *she* didn't physically favor their father, she wanted to say. She nearly asked her brother if he'd looked in a mirror lately. The older he got, he bore a distinct resemblance to R.J. Prince. The shape of his face and the perpetual frown only began the list of similarities. There was also the short cropped toffee colored, lightly graying hair but most of all, he'd inherited R.J.'s tall, muscular build – and the strength to back it up. So the next time Seth wanted to dance the "just like Pops" dance, she'd have a mirror standing by.

Seth greeted everyone guardedly except Savannah. For some inexplicable reason, he grabbed her in a hug that squeezed the breath from her. Loving, supportive words fell from his lips before he surrendered his embrace and sat down next to Dane. Savannah found herself at a loss for words. It had been a long time since Seth expressed that level of compassion. It nettled her, making her think he knew something about Ennis's condition that she didn't.

The time crept closer to the third hour and still no news. After the first hour, she grew increasingly nervous. After the third, she paced the floor, staring anxiously at the clock on the wall and watching the doors for doctors or nurses. Surely they had some news. When time closed in on the fourth hour, she sat down again, grumbling her dissatisfaction. No news is good news, Georgia and Dane assured. No news after three and a half hours of surgery spelled trouble, if anyone asked Savannah. She tuned her hearing to the subtle sounds of doctor's names being called on the PA system. Damn it, she should have taken note of the attending surgeon's name. In the back of her mind she swore it began with an "E" but her attention focused more on her sweetheart than the doctor's nametag. Besides that, a plethora of surnames barraged her over the past hours, more than one beginning with "E".

Georgia's hand covered hers. Her squeeze meant to be comforting and Savannah tried to accept it as such. She also noticed Dane's hand clasped Georgia's in a supportive gesture as well. A thought flitted through her mind, momentarily diverting her worries: Something was happening between her sister and Dane. Since he'd first visited Georgia, she noticed her sister smiling a little more, and finally laughing again. He made regular trips from Texas to spend time with Georgia. They kept to themselves for the most part, with an occasional dinner with Savannah and Ennis. Savannah stared absently at their handhold, figuring Georgia would, in time, spill her guts about the relationship. Because as stupid in love as Savannah was, she wasn't too stupid not to notice Georgia's and Dane's new found bond.

Images of Ennis crept in as her vision strayed to the Tiffany's box poking out of her purse. He spent a small fortune on her, her mind goaded, despite their agreement to not buy expensive anniversary gifts. Ennis busted that deal all to hell. Still, she couldn't get upset with him. He tried to please her, to make her smile and he effortlessly mastered it.

She removed the box, wondering about the contents. Why did Ennis choose Tiffany's over some place like Sears? Curiosity nagged at her to open the gift, to see the contents. Every month she became an eager kid about their anniversary celebration. Today, she settled for stroking the satin ribbon, leaving it in place for Ennis to present it himself. Another wave of tears threatened to surface and she closed her eyes.

"Any word on Detective Rutherford?" a male voice inquired. Savannah's eyes opened to see a uniformed officer standing in front of her.

She heaved a resigned sigh, "Nothing yet."

"We've got patrols looking for the bastard who did this. We won't rest until we've got him." His tone softened, "If there's anything you need, don't hesitate to call on us. If it's okay, a few of us are staying until we hear about Detective Rutherford's condition."

Savannah directed her attention where he pointed. "A few" in this case, consisted of a dozen or more uniformed officers filing in, rookies and veterans, men and women. Some sat in the remaining chairs in the waiting room, others chose to stand. Following them were several off duty cops. By the time the mass finished entering the room, there was little standing or sitting room available. Every head nodded once as her vision swept across each one. Astonishment adorned Dane and Georgia's features at the sheer number of officers and detectives crowding the room.

Even Savannah appeared stunned. Tears trembled in her eyes upon seeing the sight of support, "Thank you all. I know he'll appreciate it as do we."

He extended his hand gave hers a gentle shake, "We're praying for him, Detective. Remember, if you need anything, let us know."

She nodded and from the corner of her eye, she saw Dane glance at her. She assumed the reference to praying was the reason. Savannah decided years earlier that people who believed in God were simply made differently. In her younger years, she tried to be a devoted follower by praying each night before retiring to bed. Reading the Bible came as natural as a pig learning to fly but she'd tried because it pleased Charlene. Unfortunately though, having R.J. as a father hadn't exactly instilled or reinforced religious belief. He didn't go to church, didn't believe in it or God whereas Charlene did. Her mother read the Bible to all three kids, insisted they say their prayers before bedtime and took them to church when possible. No matter how unbearable life became with R.J., her mother still maintained her faith. Even when she knew she was dying, Charlene held a bond of faith stronger than steel. It was, at that time, Savannah prayed longer and harder than she had in her life. When her mother passed, a fury so hot and profound rose against God, she cursed Him and anyone who dared mention Him or prayer. Georgia found herself on the receiving end of most of the rage. While Savannah's belief vanished, her sister's rooted deeper. How, she'd asked Georgia, could she waste her time praying when it never worked? How could she still have blind faith when God ignored pleas for help? He'd taken their mother and left them alone to endure life without Charlene's love and guidance. How could she still believe?

Savannah swept away a couple of tears with her thumb. Dane offered her his hanky which brought back memories of Ennis dabbing her tears and holding her close bubbled to the surface. Ennis always had a handkerchief, most times he carried two – his blowing rag, as he called it, and a spare for unexpected occasions.

Savannah thanked Dane while touching the hanky to another drop of sadness. He patted her knee, "You've got some fine colleagues there."

"They like Ennis. He's down-to-earth and friendly. He also knows how to tone me down which they're thankful for. I get overbearing and he's good at settling that part of me." She toyed the fabric between her fingers, "He knows how to settle *every* part of me. He's my conscience, my moral support. Ennis really is my better half." She willed herself not to cry. Ennis wouldn't want her bawling so much, her little voice said. In fact, he'd probably crack some remark about dehydrating herself from crying so much. Her mind searched for another subject. Finally it hit her and she asked Dane, "Have you called your mother?"

He shook his head, "I'm holding off till after the surgery. She'll want to fly out and I don't want her panicked on the way. If she knows he's resting, she won't be such a basket case when she gets here."

Georgia gently smacked his shoulder, "Don't talk about your mother like that."

Yes, Savannah detected something more than general friendship between her sister and Dane despite Georgia's best efforts to dismiss other assumptions. For the last few months, Dane joined the choir, swearing it was all just friendly. Well, that spat on the shoulder wasn't merely friendly, Savannah thought. It had the characteristics of two people who were comfortable with one another. Very comfortable, in fact.

O O O

Another half hour passed when Georgia broached the subject, "I heard what Ennis said before going to surgery. I assumed it was the morphine playing tricks on him so I didn't mention it."

Savannah gave the clock a baleful frown, "Mention

what?"

"*Mrs.* Rutherford?"

She leaned forward, head in hands and sighed, "It wasn't the morphine. We're getting married." She checked her watch, "Don't you think we should have heard something by now? I mean, anything?" The remark about marriage rolled off her tongue with such ease it took Georgia and Dane several seconds to react. When they did she shushed them, "Don't let on you know, either." She covertly hitched her thumb toward the gaggle of officers behind them, "If the department finds out, they'll split us apart as partners and transfer one of us to another precinct."

Georgia brought her into a hug, whispering, "I'm so happy for you both, honey. It took longer than I thought but I knew Ennis would convince you."

Grinning from ear to ear, Dane winked at her with his own whisper, "Welcome to the family, Peach."

Despite the tension, she broke into her own pensive smile, "I hope he remembers when he wakes up. I've rejected marriage for so long, now I finally accept his proposal and he'll probably not remember the conversation."

"That boy may forget his own name," Dane stated with certainty, "but he'll remember that particular conversation.

Guaranteed."

Across the room a door opened. All heads lifted, waiting for a name to be called. Savannah tensed. A shorter man built like a thick tree trunk stepped out and she recognized him as the doctor who shooed her from the emergency room. She immediately started forward.

The walk seemed endless yet it only took seconds to arrive at the tiny, plain room with standing room for possibly four people and a small dog. Normally Savannah's claustrophobia kicked in hard and fast standing in a shoebox size room. Today, she only wanted to know Ennis was okay. She left Dane and Georgia behind as she rushed to the doctor. The waiting officers gathered but respectfully stood back just close enough to hear.

Savannah examined the doctor's expression. Normally judging a person's true feelings came easier. She read Ennis and Georgia like a book. With time, it gradually grew easier to identify Dane's half-truths. But the doctor possessed an impenetrable mask of ambiguity. All she recognized was a grim appearance. He didn't exactly make it easier when his vision met theirs one by one then settled on her. Savannah listened carefully while the doctor described Ennis's surgery. For all his chattering, she never heard the words "I expect him to be okay." In the meantime, she grasped certain key terms and expressions as he spoke. "We retrieved the bullet... Came very close to his heart... We'll look for any complications or infection..."

"But you expect him to be okay," she blurted, wanting an answer before she fainted at his feet. Her stomach churned, and her heart pounded in her chest. It was positively cruel to make people wait for answers, worse to force them to ask.

Dr. Etheridge hesitated which fueled her fear and temper. Savannah swallowed the gruff comment struggling for freedom. Being a cop, when she demanded answers, if they weren't provided timely enough, she found ways to pry them out. Today, however, she opted for silence while he searched for certain words, "We're hoping so, yes. After a few more days, we'll be able to tell more. For what he's been through, he's doing well."

"When can I see him?" she'd never stuttered a day in her life but rattling off simple questions seemed phenomenally difficult. The words stammered out, surprising her that anyone could actually understand her. Georgia noticed, of course, and settled a reassuring hand on her arm.

"This evening at the earliest. I want him stabilized first. I suggest you go home, eat and get some rest. He's in good hands." He bid them goodbye and walked out, leaving Savannah with her mouth open, poised for more questions.

Georgia hugged her, "Thank God. It sounds like he'll be okay."

Savannah returned the embrace and saw Dane sizing up her expression. "What's wrong?"

"He didn't say Ennis would be okay."

Her sister's brow lifted, "He sounded cautiously optimistic to me."

"He sounded vague," she argued back. They waited all day for news only to be handed elusive information. It frustrated her to be powerless. She was grateful Ennis survived the shooting and surgery. What she wanted – *needed* – to hear was he'd recover to be in her arms and in her life forever.

Suddenly she wheeled and nearly ran into Dane. He didn't step aside. Instead he caught her elbow in a firm grasp, evidently sensing her inner turmoil, "What're you doin', Peach?"

She met his vision with clear purpose, even as his fingers held secure, "I'm gonna find the bastard who did this."

"I just heard your fellow police officers say they were busy doing exactly that."

Bless Dane's heart, she thought. He acted more like a

brother to her than Seth. She loved Seth but Ennis's brother understood how to communicate with her without lighting her temper. The grip on her elbow felt far from harsh. It felt more preventative, like he protected her. His voice reinforced it, "Savannah, let them do it. They're capable and just as angry as you about what happened. Stay here and wait for Ennis."

She considered his statement. Dane was right, she knew, but feeling more helpless couldn't be achieved unless she lost control of her entire life. On second thought, she reflected, she was already there.

4

It was seven o'clock by the time she saw Ennis. In that time, Mrs. Rutherford made plans for a flight to Atlanta early the next morning. She agreed to stay with Georgia despite the fact both she and Savannah offered her a place to stay. Ennis's mother softened the refusal by telling Savannah she appreciated the offer and promised to stay with her the next trip to Atlanta. Maybe by then life would be serene on all fronts, Savannah hoped.

Mama Rutherford's decision didn't hurt her feelings. On the contrary, Georgia's house was bigger than hers. The modest two story house had two spare bedrooms whereas Savannah's smaller, single level home comfortably accommodated one. For two adults it sometimes felt cramped but Ennis never complained. Instead, he labeled it "cozy". That was Ennis, she thought to herself. Always considerate.

The doctor kept Ennis in the intensive care unit which meant only two people at a time could visit. Savannah and Dane went in first. They pushed through the swinging doors of the unit into an entirely foreign atmosphere. Beyond the polished floors and folded white linens on a cart nearby, she heard monitors beeping and nurses walking here and there, checking on patients. The patients were in small rooms, the walls made of glass for easy observation from the nurse's kiosk. Savannah counted twelve rooms in all. As they passed each one, she glanced in to see someone other than Ennis covered in a beige blanket and connected to more wires than Georgia Power and Electric.

The same sickness rose in her belly but she worked to fight it down. She felt Dane's hand on her back as he stepped toward the kiosk, inquiring softly, "Ennis Rutherford's room, please."

A stocky looking nurse who looked more like an enforcer rather than caregiver, pointed to the room across from her. Dane urged Savannah toward the open door. She felt herself push against his hand.

He whispered, "We'll help each other through this, Peach. I've got you."

She gave a subdued nod while still gathering her

courage. She'd begun to shake in those few moments, her hands trembling so bad she expected someone to notice. Savannah reverted several years to the same reaction when visiting her mother. The shaking hands, the wobbly feeling in her knees and the seed of sickness sprouting in her stomach all returned full force. Unbearable images buoyed their way to her consciousness. Charlene spent her last days in a hauntingly similar setting, comatose, struggling to live. It took an act of steel determination not to mire down in the painful memories. Ennis was now the one in the bed this time, her brain reminded, and he needed her love and support.

She and Dane stepped inside the small stark room. It was warm, nearly too warm, in her opinion. A faint beeping noise brought her attention to the machine monitoring his heart. Her vision went from toe to head, slowly taking account of her dearest friend, her loving partner, her future husband. Once her blue eyes fixed on his face, she felt weak and near breaking down again. The instinct to turn and run became overwhelming. The breathing tube in his throat robbed her of mere speech. In her mind she'd imagined him sleeping in the bed, like at home. In an instant, recollections of Charlene clawed their way back. She remembered the sound of the ventilator, the steady beeping of the heart monitor and her mother lying motionless, just as Ennis was now.

As if he sensed the turmoil raging inside her, Dane's arm tightened around her shoulders in a supportive gesture. Savannah forced a deep breath. No matter how intense the urge to flee, she would stay as she had with her mother. Her love for Ennis was too strong to entertain the alternative.

She stepped closer to the bed as did Dane. From the corner of her eye, she saw Dane watching her. He spoke first, "Hey, bro. Look who I found loitering in the hallway."

Savannah swallowed dryly, gathering her nerve. She took his hand in hers and held it to her cheek, surprised at how warm he felt. His large hand engulfed hers, his long, meaty fingers limp in her grasp. She bent to kiss his forehead, "Hey there, baby," she said. "I'm here, Dane and Georgia are too and your mama's coming to see you. Bobby called from Augusta, said he'd be here tomorrow."

"And you've got a hallway full of police officers waiting out there too," Dane added. "Popular fella."

She thought she saw his brow twitch as they spoke as if he wanted to reply but couldn't. "Give yourself a little time and you'll be good as new," she said. "Then you can decide where we go on our honeymoon." She didn't think his brow twitched this time. She knew it did. Ennis's facial movements indicated a level of consciousness that gave her a flame of hope.

Dane's brow also lifted and he glanced at her, "That got his juices flowing."

She chanced a smile and kissed Ennis's hand, "You have to get well first, babe. Doctors frown on honeymoon activities unless you're fully healed." She felt tears mounting at his expressive attempts to respond. Her voice held soft and steady, "We've got a lot of years ahead of us, Ennis. Every one of them as husband and wife."

O O O

On the ride from the airport, Georgia still marveled at Savannah's description of Mama Rutherford. It was dead on. Mrs. Rutherford looked eerily similar to Ellie Ewing from "Dallas". The weirdest part was she even acted like her. To quote Savannah, Mama was "as close to Ellie Ewing as nature dared". Her rounded middle told of a woman who loved to cook and enjoyed indulging but not to excess. Her hair sported streaks of gray styled into a replication of the TV character, her face had a soft, natural kindness that Georgia instantly recognized in Ennis. Even Dane inherited warm, smiling eyes from their mother. But beneath the pleasant, grandmotherly appearance Georgia detected a card carrying Steel Magnolia. She noticed it when they'd spoken on the phone around Christmas. Depending on the situation, Mama displayed leadership, love and support, all characteristics of a good mother. They all needed a woman like Mama Rutherford and Georgia had a feeling she needed just as much support from them.

After she and Dane loaded his mother's luggage into the Tahoe and updated Mrs. Rutherford on Ennis's condition, the older woman climbed in beside Georgia and got down to business, "How's Savannah doing?"

As if on cue, both Dane and Georgia proceeded to explain nothing short of dynamite would blast her from Ennis's side. Not unlike a military general being briefed on troop movements, Mama listened in detail as one or the other described how Savannah wouldn't eat or take time to rest. She stayed with Ennis, talking to him, telling jokes or reading from his collection of western novels. "Don't know what'll give out first. Her or her voice," Dane finished.

His mother rode in silence for about a mile then, "Will she eat if it's brought to her?"

Georgia pulled off the highway and onto a side street. She'd tried to avoid the noon traffic by exiting early and taking a lesser used route. Judging by the traffic, that too was a mistake, "Not if it takes her away from Ennis."

"And she's not eaten in over a day?"

It was Dane's turn to answer, "Nope."

The first spark of Mama Rutherford's grit ignited, "That girl needs a meal and rest. Georgia, honey, do you live close by?"

"I live closer to the hospital than she does."

"If you don't mind, after I see Ennis, I'll drop by and prepare a little meal for her."

Georgia relaxed a bit behind the wheel. She was glad Mrs. Rutherford was here. Savannah needed a mother figure right now. She'd tried to guide and support her little sister and got snarled at for her trouble. During their childhood only Charlene managed the inconceivable. Savannah only listened to their mother. Now, with Mama Rutherford, an older woman Savannah respected and loved, Georgia prayed her sister listened to Ennis's mother like she listened to theirs.

Dane forewarned Georgia to address his mother as "Mama." His mother understood formalities and appreciated them but, he explained, the Prince girls were family to her and nothing short of "Mama" would do. Georgia had to re-gear her brain as, she assumed, Savannah did too. They'd both called their mother "Mama" and calling another woman by the name would take adjustment. "Mama," she said, "if you can pry her out of there, I'll be most happy to fix everyone's supper." She hated to mention it but also worried the men's mother would be blindsided by Savannah's worst trait, "She does have a bad temper so you might prepare yourself."

Mama chuckled, undeterred, "That's okay, honey. I've got one too. She may get angry with me but I'll win the argument."

Mama sounded confident enough however Georgia grew up with Savannah's fierce disposition. At times, she'd bet her little sister could scare the devil into submission. Georgia took note of the time: Noon. The unit was staffed with a different crew of nurses than last night. Those folks got a rude awakening when they tried running Savannah out after visiting hours. Her temper turned so fiery they feared getting burned. The problem with Savannah, Georgia grimly remembered, was the more weariness set in, the grumpier she got. If Mama Rutherford couldn't pry her kid sister loose, Georgia feared she'd be banned from seeing Ennis due to her temper.

Once they arrived at the hospital, Georgia gave Mama one last caution about her sister's temperament. The older woman patted her hand reassuringly, "She'll be fine."

Georgia flinched. She dreaded seeing the scene unfold but escorted the woman into ICU anyway. As she suspected, Savannah hadn't moved from Ennis's side. A book laid open across her lap, her reading glasses remained perched on her nose and as they neared, Georgia heard her reading to Ennis.

The stress and fatigue wore heavy in Savannah's features. Georgia feared Ennis's situation would extend into long exhaustive days and weeks, maybe even months. Her sister's staying power already waned. Georgia couldn't allow herself to think what Savannah would be like after another week.

Mama paused and watched. "She's not left once?"

Georgia shook her head, "She won't leave him. She lets others visit but when they leave she's right back in there."

Mama padded quietly toward Ennis's room. Georgia followed, hoping Ennis's mother could talk sense into her sister. Mama stepped inside at the same time Savannah looked up. The relieved expression lasted only moments as she rose, Ennis's hand still in hers. Mama enfolded her in a loving embrace, "Savannah, honey, you look so tired."

Georgia held her breath, waiting for the firestorm to begin. Any hint of asking her to leave and Savannah bared her claws. Georgia mentioned she looked weary earlier but her sister backed her off with a fearsome scowl, especially when Georgia stated she should go home and get some sleep.

Surprisingly, as she removed her glasses, Savannah suppressed the scowl for Mama Rutherford and settled for a small nod, "A little but I'm okay. He's settled in, I think. They've got him on morphine right now. He seems to be comfortable."

"Well, is it any wonder with his sweetheart by his side? Honestly, honey, Georgia told me you haven't had a morsel to eat or even a nap. Why don't you take a little break? I'll be right here with him."

Georgia saw her sister tense, a reaction that Mama countered, "I promise if anything changes I'll call you. Georgia says she lives close by so staying there would be fine. You're a hop, skip and a jump from Ennis."

The beginnings of a tiny smile floated to the surface. Georgia figured it revolved around Mama's colloquialism. One day in Atlanta and Mrs. Rutherford would realize nothing was a mere hop, skip and a jump from anywhere. The older woman patted Savannah's back as though the decision were made, "I've got your phone number and Georgia said she could whip up a quick meal then you can steal forty winks. I know my boy's in good hands with you, honey, but you need a break and I'm here to provide it."

Savannah ran her fingers through her hair and sighed, "Mama, I'm fine, really. I appreciate your concern though."

Georgia's brow arched in disbelief at Savannah's pleasantness. Anyone else approaching her would slink away bleeding. A peaceful calm eased the lines in the older sister's features. Help was here and her name was Mama.

Mama Rutherford cupped Savannah's cheek, "I know you're a dedicated girl or my son wouldn't love you so much but you'll make *me* feel better if you get some food and rest."

At this point Savannah looked to her sister who presented her own tired smile. The female detective hugged Mama again, thanked her and proceeded to trudge in Georgia's direction.

5

Hell of a lot of good this does. I could be at the hospital with Ennis...
Savannah turned in the bed again, a loud sigh punctuating her
frustration. Mama Rutherford meant well, she realized that.
From the moment they met, she seemed to take Savannah under
her maternal wing as her own. Savannah didn't object since his
mother reminded her somewhat of Charlene.

She left Ennis with his mother not because she wanted to
leave but because she realized Mama needed time with her son.
Savannah spent time alone with Ennis, it was only fair that his
mother did too. She'd never tell Mama but it was that reason
alone that convinced her to leave, not the older woman's
diplomacy about food and rest.

Georgia rivaled Julia Child in the kitchen yet the
casserole remained essentially bland to Savannah. It smelled
heavenly and she was sure at any other time the meal's taste

would have reflected it. She wanted to please her sister by eating a hearty meal. After all, she'd spent an hour on the preparation itself but Savannah mostly picked around the casserole. Worries consumed her about Ennis. Worries with no solutions. Savannah felt utterly powerless, a situation she rarely experienced and one that robbed her emotional stability. Between worrying, battling the desire to hunt down the shooter, and the intrinsic need to bawl, her hours were decidedly filled.

When she noticed her sister policing her food intake, she consumed a bite or two, ensuring Georgia witnessed it. Afterward, the eldest encouraged – essentially insisted – Savannah retire upstairs for some sleep.

Savannah capitulated like a good little sister, despite the knowledge any attempt to sleep was destined for failure. She reached for her watch on the nightstand. For an hour she'd fought the covers, her thoughts and memories, and her inner pain. Closing her eyes brought images of a faceless suspect lifting a gun and pulling the trigger. Ennis stood wide eyed, paralyzed as the bullet sped from the gun and pierced his chest. She watched him clutch the wound, blood spilling between his fingers as he collapsed to his knees…

"Need something to help you sleep?" a voice asked, pulling her from the vision. She saw Georgia at the doorway, concern etched deep in her brow.

Savannah blinked, realizing tears dampened the pillow. She swiped her cheeks with her hand, "Whatever it is won't help me rest but thanks."

Georgia padded in the room and sat on the side of the bed. She swept her sister's dark waves back, "You're gonna have to sleep sometime, hon. Ennis knows you love him. That will bring him through this."

What a nice thought, that love could change fate. Had it been true Ennis would be at home with her, not at the hospital clinging to life. "Why didn't I marry him sooner? Why did I keep pushing him away?"

Georgia chanced a gentle smile, "You were scared. You thought everything would change for the worst if you got married. Truth is, I think you and Ennis will make it just fine together."

"If he lives, you mean. I've..." she hesitated to continue. The subject had been a bone of contention between the sisters for years. If mentioning God sparked another heated debate, Savannah promised never to speak of Him again. In retrospect, the wisest decision was keeping quiet. "Nothin'."

Georgia encouraged her to continue, "You've what? It's important or you wouldn't have brought it up."

"I've been praying for him." She wanted to say it fast and painless. It surfaced slower, guarded. With the admission, she expected Georgia to pounce around the room singing the Hallelujah Chorus. Instead, her sister's touch went from her hair to her back, her soft smile growing slightly bigger, "That's good. Ennis needs us all to pray for him. May I ask why the change?"

"You can blame Dane. He insisted I try again."

Georgia patted her back, "Good for Dane. I'll have to thank him."

Savannah pointedly made eye contact, "I'm not a convert yet. If God pulls off a miracle, then you can thank Dane."

o   o   o

After two agonizing days of worrying and waiting, Savannah began to wonder what God had against her. She never professed to be a good child, but she didn't believe Ennis should suffer for her shortcomings – if that's the way God worked. Georgia assured her it wasn't.

Savannah decided to go casual in an Atlanta Thrashers sweatshirt and jeans. The days were warm, nearly to the point of oppressing, but she'd spent the better part of her time freezing since Ennis's shooting. Besides, she thought, Ennis wouldn't care what she wore when he woke up – *if* he woke up.

She sat with her sister, Seth and his wife Leah, Dane and Mama Rutherford, still waiting for an update on Ennis's progress that morning. The doctor visited mid-morning every day then close to five in the evening. The nurses shooed everyone into the waiting room while the doctor checked Ennis over.

It equated to Chinese Water torture, Savannah thought disgustedly. By now Ennis should have shown signs of improving or waking up. Hospital staff threw the words "it takes time" around to the point her head threatened to explode. Something wasn't right and patience wasn't working and all her prayers went unanswered. That was, until a familiar face appeared at the waiting room door.

The officer that initially drove her to the hospital stepped inside the sparsely populated waiting room. He seemed ill at ease much like the day he informed her of the shooting. After hesitantly studying the assembled group, Officer Meade nervously meandered closer, "Detective, I need to speak with you."

Savannah nodded, excused herself. He led her a few feet away to a remote corner. His vision shifted to the side, a move she read as concern they'd be overheard. Rookies assumed everything was a highly protected secret so she took a breath and urged him to spill it, "What is it?"

The family focused on the nervous cop, probably more than necessary because of his behavior. He fidgeted his uniform cap between his hands and finally leaned in, whispering, "They caught the bastard who shot Detective Rutherford."

Disregarding the family's sudden interest behind her, Savannah felt the blood rising inside, her temper swelling to volcanic proportions, "You're sure it's him?"

Meade still glanced at the others. Seth and Dane had leaned forward, elbows on knees, to eavesdrop. The officer leaned closer, whispering, "Yes, ma'am. Witnesses confirmed it's him."

Oblivious to the conversation's extra participants, Savannah drew a deep breath, her voice not as covert at Meade's, "He's at our station?"

The cop nodded once, his eyes roaming the group but settling on Dane and Seth, "Detective Mathis is the lead on the investigation. He wanted me to update you."

"Thanks," she returned to her seat, fixated on her new goal. The opportunity she craved for days finally arrived. Hell, it came *gift-wrapped* with its own personal messenger. She grabbed her purse. "I gotta go for a while. Tell Ennis I'll be back shortly."

Seth seized her wrist, "We've had to pry you from his side since this happened and now you're running off? Where are you going?"

"Never you mind," she cautioned. She saw Seth's vision narrow slightly. Besides being talked down to, he hated being dismissed. But since this gem of news fell in her lap, she'd die before allowing anyone to stop her. She had to make things right – for Ennis.

O   O   O

After fifteen minutes of weaving through traffic and blasting through red lights, the Camaro came to a screeching stop at the entrance of the station. Savannah reached in the glove compartment for her .38 and badge. After equipping herself with both, she exited the car, marched to the building and threw open the door.

The sergeant on duty inquired about Ennis only to receive silence in return. Savannah focused on a single objective: to meet the son of a bitch who shot her partner. Her stormy features and purposeful strides warded off extraneous questions or comments from coworkers. The station buzzed with news of the arrest. Through the haze of rage she caught key words to various conversations – conversations that ceased instantly when the speakers noticed her presence. She strode down the hallway then turned until coming to the interview rooms.

A rookie cop stood guard by one and upon catching her eye, the young man wilted. Glancing through the window, she saw a transient-looking man in his late twenties sitting at the desk, handcuffed. She pointed to the door, "Is that him?"

The general reference to the suspect would become a ritual performed throughout the city that day. By end of shift, every cop in town would know Ennis's shooter was in custody and they would refer to the suspect merely as "him".

Even the rookie Lawson cowering before her knew the law enforcement grapevine sparked to life as seconds ticked on. "Y-yes, ma'am," he stammered. "Detective Mathis was questioning him earlier."

She pushed her sleeves back, "It's my turn now. Step aside."

For a young man barely a month on the job, Lawson recognized the importance of his present task. She saw him battling the quandary of allowing her inside. The two knew each other on a friendly basis as she'd freely advised him on certain particulars of police policy, some the academy taught, some not. Being a rookie tested all a person's emotions and limits in a short amount of time. A handful of people struggled with the job until they had a few years behind them. She certainly did, so when the department assigned a new rookie to the station, Savannah attempted to ease the transition by offering advice unlike Detective Mathis who preferred the scolding method. Mathis, ten years her senior, initiated her in his Archie Bunker style. Her first day as a detective, he took her aside warning, "Don't go screwin' up. The fallout don't just hit you, it hits us all." From that moment, she made herself a promise to enlighten rookies – and new detectives – with finesse, not a brick.

Lawson's mouth worked but no sound came out. It became obvious he didn't want to refuse her but he sure hated to endure Detective John Mathis if he didn't. "Detective, I don't think this is a good idea…"

Savannah was tired of playing nice. The hospital staff refused to provide an honest opinion about Ennis, her family slowly and unceremoniously seized the reigns to her life so she wasn't about to be rejected by a rookie. Opening the door, she leveled an icy glare on the kid, backing him off but not without his final caution, "But you're not supposed to bring your weapon –"

Halfway through his statement, she'd closed the door, leaving him to mumble the remaining words. No, police officers weren't allowed to bring their weapons into the interview room. As of late, however, she wasn't feeling like a civil servant. She experienced the rage she'd seen from families whose loved one fell victim to homicide. The anger slipped in so easily and it quickly boiled into a murderous fury. She understood why families literally screamed at her for justice and why they vowed to avenge their loved one's death. Savannah physically fought and restrained countless family members from plunging into a life changing mistake – what she labeled a mistake at the time. She'd wrestled knives from mothers and guns from fathers and brothers. Woe be unto the fool who tangled with her today, she told herself. She had a mission and intended to follow through, no matter what the cost.

The pungent stench of body odor hung so heavily in the room it turned her stomach but she managed to swallow back the sickness. She reached up and slid the deadbolt in place, locking the two inside.

Taking a breath, Savannah turned to face the man she likened to Satan. His long dirty blond hair hung in tangled strings across his shoulders. A scraggly growth of beard covered his cheeks indicating he'd not only forgone the bath but the razor as well – probably for several weeks. Tattoos of dragons adorned his forearms, skulls smiled from his biceps. The man wore dirty torn jeans and a sky blue t-shirt with several holes ripped in it. Her vision instantly locked on shirt. Spatters of blood dotted the front. Ennis's blood. The sight topped off Savannah's rage, making it practically impossible to control her trembling hands. She wanted to make this asshole suffer and that's exactly what she intended to do.

Making eye contact with him, she was surprised at his relaxed posture. He stretched, declaring, "I told the other cop, I ain't saying a word. Not without a lawyer."

She stepped closer, "You don't need a lawyer for what I'm here for."

This amused the man and his mouth curled into a presumptuous smile. His cuffed hands patted his crotch, "Come on, darlin'. If you're the dish for today, serve somethin' up."

Angered beyond rational thought, she unclipped her badge and slammed it on the table, bringing his eyes wide open

- and not with desire. When she withdrew her .38 from the holster and also laid it on the table, his vision lifted to hers. "I'm afraid," she began, "the menu's limited today, especially when I see a cop's blood on someone's shirt."

He leaned back in the chair, "That ain't no cop's blood." He wisecracked, "I cut myself shaving." He punctuated his statement by brushing a hand down his cheek.

His smartass remark further infuriated her. She circled around to his back. Her temper flared, her palm drew back and put every ounce of strength into whacking the back of his head. The force propelled him forward until his hands braced against the table. The unexpected attack brought him to his feet, "Bitch, you'll regret doin' that."

Savannah shoved him into the seat with surprising force, "Sit down, asshole." She fisted a thick clump of hair and snapped his head back, directing his vision to hers, "Unless you're confessing, shut your mouth 'cause this bitch doesn't like liars and bastards who shoot cops."

He flinched and wormed from the pain but still presented an aloof posture, "I didn't shoot nobody and you can't treat me like this. It's against the law."

Savannah slammed his face into the metal table so violently, it echoed through the room, "I'll tell you what's *against the law*, asshole. Gunning down cops. That was my partner you shot. He was *my partner.*" She yanked his head back again, unimpressed by the sight of his bloody nose and lip. She was, however, impressed with the fear in his eyes as she spoke, "I want your full, undivided attention and I don't believe I have it." She smashed his face into the tabletop again, a resounding clang echoed through the small room. She lifted his head, mildly satisfied with the spray of blood left on the table, "Now maybe I do. Since you get your jollies shooting cops, here's what we're gonna do. We're playing a game together." She used her free hand to slide her gun closer to him. She felt him pull away from the weapon but her hold tensed in his hair, "We're gonna see who can reach this gun faster. Whoever does gets to shoot the loser."

His cuffed hands waved as if warding off evil spirits, "You're crazy. You can't do this." He repeated in a way that he sincerely hoped that, "Cops can't do this."

A buzz of panicked male voices behind the locked door warned Savannah her time with the shooter gradually ran out. Outside the room, questions were volleyed at the young rookie who, when he answered, sounded pretty frightened himself. She heard two voices in particular call her name: Her captain and her brother. The latter briefly splintered her anger. What was Seth doing here? Resentment bolstered her fury with the realization he'd followed her to the station.

Seth, his tone verging on panic, yelled for her to open the door. Her brother knew the capacity of her temper and also knew how much she loved Ennis.

Her captain's voice, on the other hand, sounded downright pissed off, "Prince, whatever you're thinking, don't do it! Open up and get your ass out here now!"

She had to work fast before they forced their way inside. Between the asshole in front of her and the men outside wanting to stop her, it became more difficult to mask her fury. She grabbed the chain linking the handcuffs and pulled the suspect's hands toward the table, "Reach for it."

"No," he pushed as far away from the weapon as possible. The utterance of the word positively infuriated Savannah. By God, he *would* reach for that gun if she had to manhandle him to do it. She tightened her grip in his hair and jerked his head back to face her, "Reach for it now, you miserable bastard, or you forfeit the game. That means I win and your next stop is the morgue."

The man flinched at the pain. He pulled against her hand, wrestling to free himself, "Someone help me! This bitch is gonna kill me!"

She smiled a bitter, angry smile, "Maybe you're not so stupid after all."

During her career, homicidal feelings emerged toward certain suspects but she managed to curb them, mostly by running it off. She strived to control that part of herself. All cops did but everyone had a breaking point and she'd long surpassed hers. Even as her vision passed across the two-way mirror to her own reflection, she stared back at a stranger. The recesses of her brain forewarned of the line she was about to cross. Rage pushed the voice away, smothering it in a lethal mixture of revenge and hate.

She grabbed the gun and thrust the barrel under the suspect's jaw, the pressure steadily increasing. He cried another plea for help to which she replied, "No one here will help you. You shot one of us, dumbshit. If I didn't kill you, one of them would."

A thunderous crack commanded their immediate attention. Someone began kicking in the door. Savannah grasped the .38 hard, her forefinger started squeezing the trigger as another solid blow resonated through the room. This time she didn't look. Neither did the suspect. His vision riveted on hers, his trembling voice pleading, "Don't do it. Please don't kill me."

She crushed the words between clenched teeth, "You shouldn't have shot my best friend." Her finger was halfway home when something, rather some*one*, jarred her stance forward, removing the immediate threat for the suspect. Savannah struggled to remain on her feet as a blur of arms and hands attempted to subdue her and retrieve the gun.

The room spun for a moment until she crashed against the jail cell in the room. Behind her she heard a smattering of voices. The most distinct, the closest, belonged to her brother, "Sorry about that, sis. You okay?"

Did he *really* ask that ludicrous question? She balanced her words but not very carefully, "I won't be okay until that bastard's dead." She struggled against his hold, expending every ounce of fight in her. "Let me go!" Evidently it was Seth's arm around her waist and his hand gripping her gun hand. Both tightened as his concerned mood faded to frustration, "Van, stop fighting me. Just let the gun go."

Someone restrained her left hand from punching at the intruders. It was Dane. He held firm but not as hard as Seth, "Give it up, girl. This isn't the way to help Ennis."

Savannah struggled against both in a wild, frantic battle. The bitter pain of reliving Ennis's nightmare surged adrenaline through her, giving her more strength. The image of her partner clinging to life drove her struggle and for the first time in her life, she gained the upper hand on her brother.

Everyone in the room realized the two men were losing their fight. Almost in unison she heard three voices shout, "The gun!"

Savannah twisted from Seth's hold and took dead aim on the suspect. This time the blow came not from Seth but from her captain. His large hand clamped down on her wrist at the same time he bulled her against the wall. She managed to turn her face away just before her body crashed into the concrete. The impact knocked the breath from her, refocusing her thoughts on merely obtaining air in her lungs. The weight of Hunter's muscular body crushed her but also effectively immobilized her. This time no apology was offered from the man behind her, "Drop the gun or you go into the cell next to this son of a bitch. Then you won't see Ennis for a long time." To emphasize his order, he solidified his grasp on her wrist and twisted until she whimpered.

Somehow the weapon's appeal diminished with the pain shooting up her wrist to her shoulder. She released the gun to Seth's custody who then handed it to an officer. Captain Hunter kept steady pressure on her arm, "I don't know what's prompted you to this drastic measure but I can assure you your career is on the line. When I release you, you'd better stand down."

Savannah continued to writhe until he tweaked her wrist again, "Prince, do you hear me? Stand down." When he received no answer, he addressed the officers, "Take him downstairs and outta her sight."

She heard a scuffle behind her and realized her opportunity was slipping away. From the corner of her eye, she saw the man smile. Her rage resurfaced, "Don't think you're safe, you bastard. I don't care how long it takes, I'll hunt you down and kill you for shooting him. Do you hear me? I'll kill you!" Savannah strained against Josh's hold and got a reinforcing nudge as his annoyance mounted, "You're one step away from wearing a pair of matching silver bracelets."

"Let me go," she growled.

Dane and her brother surrounded her, blocking her way out as well as the uniform's access to her. If they thought merely standing in her way discouraged her, they thought wrong. The instant Hunter's grasp loosened, she launched herself between both men. What she hadn't counted on was their quick reflexes. Both Seth and Dane locked their arms through hers only to experience another round of her ire. This time it was Dane who snaked his arm around her waist,

"Savannah, he's gone. Settle down, girl. *Please.*"

Hunter withdrew a set of cuffs from his belt. The sight of them tensed her for yet another battle. For the first time in her life, she saw her brother flustered beyond words. Through his labored breathing, he hastily sought the key to diffuse the situation. He finally opted for addressing Hunter, "Hold off on those. Let me talk to her."

The captain tilted his chin and crossed his arms, clearly skeptical of Seth's idea but agreed to wait.

Seth didn't make the mistake of standing in front of her. He obviously sensed the fact she'd do nearly anything to get her hands on the shooter, even mowing down relatives. He did, however, join Dane's attempts at calming her, "Van, you're not doing Ennis any good by acting this way." He leaned closer, mumbling, "You don't want to lose your job and you sure don't want to go to jail."

She had the perfect comeback, at least for the former. It poised itself precariously on her lips even as Captain Josh Hunter filled her vision, his arms still folded over his chest, his brow sinking toward Hell. A uniformed officer handed him the badge she'd laid on the table before confronting the suspect.

She struggled against Dane and her brother. Dane wrapped his other arm across her chest, essentially bracing her against him. She glared at Josh who returned the favor but added, "You're walking a thin line to losing these," he held up the badge and gun.

Her blue eyes narrowed as she wielded each syllable like a hammer, "Far as I'm concerned, you can keep 'em. All they managed to do for Ennis was get him shot."

O O O

Dane felt utterly crappy and according to her brother's expression, he felt about the same. Neither had wanted the encounter to end the way it had. The surprised look she gave them when she realized they were present twisted his gut. When he and Seth heard the officer at the hospital explain they had the suspect in custody, they knew Savannah would probably go after him. The two men rode in Seth's truck, tearing out and keeping up with the Camaro (a feat in itself) then tried to follow Savannah into the station. They'd only gotten so far when officers refused their access to the interview rooms. Only when they explained the situation did the cops understand their panic.

During the scuffle, uniformed officers and detectives alike clogged the hallway, all vying for a view of the action. A smattering of reactions registered on their faces from wide-eyed shock to angered determination. It reminded Dane of an after-school brawl with gangs of kids rooting for one side or the other, only this time, the whole gang rooted for the infuriated female loose in the interview room.

Now, after the fireworks, the hallways cleared, leaving a few stragglers to witness Hunter threaten Savannah with her job and her basically instruct him where to stick it. To everyone else, she just looked damn mad. To Dane, he realized how close she was to breaking down. She slowly relaxed in his hold and he chanced releasing her. God bless, for such a tall, lanky girl, she possessed the strength of an ox. Dane highly underestimated the fight in Ennis's partner and his muscles were telling him about it. He watched Savannah square off with Captain Hunter, a man Dane would likely think twice about confronting.

Hunter considered her verbal overreaction but only momentarily, "Savannah, I know how you feel about Ennis."

"No, you don't," was her defensive reply.

Josh bristled, his vision narrowing the longer he remained silent. Dane saw recognition in Hunter's features. He knew or believed Savannah and Ennis were closer than partners on the job.

Hunter waved the .38 in front of her, "I *do* know that barging in here and trying to off the suspect is so over the top for you, I'm beginning to think you lost your marbles."

By this time, both Dane and Seth released her and she stood quietly for the most part. Dane watched her rub her head with the heel of her hand. He'd be surprised if her head didn't pound as wild and irate as she'd been. Her hands shook as though the gravity of the last few moments finally took their toll.

With one hand, Dane pulled out a chair, his voice gentle, "Sit down, Peach."

Savannah shook her head, "I'm okay."

No, she wasn't, he wanted to say but thought better of it. Her face verged on crimson instead of the plum from minutes earlier and her hands still trembled from the adrenaline rush. Josh's hands braced her shoulders, guiding her to the chair. Dane felt her tense at her captain's touch. He certainly couldn't blame her. The tackle Josh laid on her would have taken the drive out of a Mack truck.

"Savannah, sit down," Hunter instructed in a voice much kinder than what he'd used minutes previously.

She refused to meet anyone's gaze but Dane sensed her wrestling with the rage and disappointment. Since the physical struggle ended, the anger ebbed slightly, leaving the frustration weighing heavier. Instead of following orders, she marched out with a resolve that told all present to go to hell.

The group of men stood stunned. Hunter, on the other hand, watched her tramp down the hall of his station house. Dane sensed the battle wasn't over. Hunter's fists repeatedly clenched and released until he finally unleashed his own temper, "Prince!"

Not only Savannah's momentum stopped, a few passing cops also halted in their tracks. Hunter's expression and tone withered every nearby cop except her. She turned on her heel and for the first time Dane saw indifference in her expression.

Hunter whipped a pointing finger toward an empty room, "In my office now."

Dane never once doubted her affection for his brother but damn, he hadn't realized what a spitfire she was. If he wanted a fiercely protective partner and wife for Ennis, he got it in spades. Their mama would've been impressed. Scared out of her mind but impressed. Even squaring off with her captain, she showed no outward signs of backing down or splintering into a million tears.

She pursed her lips, stalked to the small office. Dane prayed she'd reconsider her words. Quitting the police department after so many years and the commendations she'd received wasn't a normally intelligent move. Still, Dane understood her anger. Ennis was shot doing a good deed, being a good cop.

He watched Savannah stride rod straight into Hunter's office. She stood deathly still, waiting and stewing while the captain shut the door. While Dane and Seth migrated toward the office, Seth decided to call Georgia to update her. Expelling a long sigh, Seth wiped his brow while punching numbers with his thumb. Dane wholeheartedly agreed. Witnessing that scene could have sapped the strength from Hercules. Dane heard her brother describe the whole bizarre scene, wait for Georgia's reply then reply, "Forget the job. We're just grateful she's not locked up."

They remained a respectable distance, Dane tuned his hearing to listen. The captain spoke too low to hear as he presented her with her badge and gun. Dane willed her to take them. Instead, she stood motionless.

Hunter sat them on his desk then leaned against it, arms crossed. Savannah never spoke but her vision scanned the squad room, ready to take on any clod stupid enough to look in her general direction. From Dane's estimate, he counted about ten people in line for a lashing from her, twelve including him and Seth. Business in the squad ground to a deafening halt while Hunter cornered Savannah in his office.

Dane heard whispers behind him. They consisted of various disciplinary actions their captain could slap on his female detective – if she managed to keep her job. Moments passed and more cops appeared. They joined the conversations while keeping a cautious eye to Hunter's office. Some expressed sympathy for her, one saying, "Shoulda let her kill the bastard. He deserves it."

Once one person gathered courage to speak, the others eased into hushed conversations as well. "Yeah," another chimed in, this one bolder, louder with his tone, "coulda had that son of a bitch tried, convicted and executed in five minutes."

Undaunted one other uniform cop slanted Dane and Seth a narrow glance, "Who are they anyway? They're not even cops."

Dane felt his own anger rising even as Seth answered, "I'm her brother," and left it at that. Dane fisted his hands and turned, ready to set the record straight for his part, "I'm Ennis Rutherford's brother. I yanked her out because if my brother survives this, it would destroy him to know she'd ruined her life and career by killing that bastard."

That seemed to shut them all up – or it could have been the muted sound of Savannah's voice then Hunter's louder, incensed tone, "Damn it, Savannah, don't tell me to keep them again or I'm liable to do it. It may be out of my hands anyway. This may take a road I can't help you with. I'll do what I can but –"

"Don't bother. Losing Ennis is the worst that could happen so anything this department does to me can't compare."

Her words spurred Hunter rod straight like she. He towered over her, his face fire red, his finger redirecting itself to her face, "You're not in your right mind because of this situation and I'm cutting you more slack than any superior should. Take a moment to think how special cops are treated in prison. If you'd succeeded in killing him –"

"You should have let me! Someone has to –"

"Shut up and let me finish!" Hunter's voice boomed from the office, "I've known you since your rookie days and seen you through plenty of scrapes. You've never acted this crazy or preached vigilantism." He took a breath and lowered his tone. He spoke softly, forcing Dane to strain to hear. He noticed Seth also leaned in, cocked his ear to the door as Hunter continued, "I know you and Ennis are close. Is there something going on between you?"

Dane held his breath, waiting for Savannah's reply. According to Hunter's reaction she hedged on the answer which further exasperated the captain, "Nevermind. I have my own suspicions."

Dane swallowed hard, reinforcing his courage before softly knocking on the door. Hunter's vision lifted to see him then waved him in. Savannah glanced at Dane briefly, the anger replaced with more exhaustion than anything. Dane extended his hand to Josh, "Dane Rutherford, Ennis's brother."

Josh's sight went from Dane to Savannah then back, recognition blossoming in his expression as he introduced himself and shook hands, "Now I realize why you pulled her out instead of my officers."

Dane chanced a tiny smile, "I figured it was best for Ennis to beat me up for manhandling his partner instead of subjecting your troops to it." He saw the corners of her mouth lift slightly, then her chin trembled as emotions began overwhelming her again. She turned to the window to avoid anyone seeing the tears.

He slid his arm around her shoulders, "Actually I was hoping to intervene on Savannah's behalf. She and my brother are pretty close."

Hunter's vision narrowed slightly, as he zeroed in on his

detective, "I suspected that, yes."

"I think she needs a little time to cool off, rest up and see my brother through this. If she doesn't take the badge back yet, could you keep it for her? Because she *will* be back."

Again, Josh crossed his arms, waiting for an argument from his detective. Savannah didn't speak for or against the idea. At least she'd cooled down enough not to fight about the job. Dane was thankful.

Hunter rubbed his jaw, studying her posture, her hand gently dabbing a tear here and there, "I'd really hate to lose Savannah. She's proven herself to be a good detective. I was keeping the offer open anyway but I'm hoping you'll be able to talk sense into her." Josh reached out, his hand taking hers, "Take care of Ennis. Get him through this then come see me. When he's ready, he can do the same."

Savannah's cell phone rang consequently ending the current conversation. She eyed the Caller ID, and Dane noticed the panic flooding her features. "It's Georgia." She clicked on without greeting her sister, "What's wrong?"

The gnawing grew in the pit of Dane's stomach too. Something *was* wrong with Ennis. The instinctive need to be with his brother pulled at him. He prayed the meeting was over so Seth could drive him back to the hospital. Each second that ticked by escalated his anxiousness.

The men listened closer, and Seth moved to the door. Savannah's expression combined resolve with beginning tears, "I'll be right there." She clicked off without the usual farewell gestures the sisters signed off with.

Savannah clipped the phone back on her belt and headed for the door, "Ennis is going back into surgery. Internal bleeding."

She tried to push past her brother but Seth braced her by the shoulders, "I'll drive you." He nodded to Dane who bid farewell to Josh Hunter. Hunter, on the other hand, offered, "I'll drive. I'll drive her and Dane in a detective's car. We'll get there fast and without any arguments from patrol units."

6

Savannah stood over the flag draped casket, expecting tears to well in her eyes. It surprised her they didn't. Numbness overwhelmed the pain, as she guessed happened at times like this. The mind could endure only so much. The condolences, the endless funeral procession stretching for miles through Atlanta metro, and the mass of blue uniforms flooding the cemetery – so many people yet she felt alone. Her family supported her and loved her but she only wanted Ennis back. For now, she would float in the numbness, knowing that some day soon, the pain would return because he couldn't.

Hundreds of faceless officers, from beat cops to the chief of police, crowded the lush grass area around Ennis's grave. Savannah just counted herself as one of them, in her dress blues adorned with her breast bar commendations and shield, the latter covered with a black band across it.

Civilians dressed for the hot, sweltering weather. Most were family, his and hers. Both bunched together as one group. She thought that odd. She thought it particularly odd that she stood alone at the casket while others comforted each other. Had she chosen to isolate herself? She couldn't remember.

Savannah stood motionless during the playing of "Taps". Crying became an obsession now. Why couldn't she cry? Everyone else – Georgia, Ennis's mother, his sister-in-law Bobbi and countless others spilled tears like a river. Her eyes, however, remained dry and no manner of willing herself to cry brought moisture to them.

Stationed several yards away, the honor guard in their dress blue uniforms and pristine white gloves slowly lifted rifles to their shoulders for a twenty-one gun salute.

The numbness suddenly faded, giving way to sorrow. Savannah's heart ached so deeply she gritted her teeth to bear the pain. "God never puts more on you than you can bear," Grandma Culberson had said many years ago. She's also ended it with, "But He sure can bend you double sometimes." While the honor guard prepared for their salute, Savannah prayed to God for strength. She begged him to lift the pain and guilt that crippled her. "God help me please. I need you," she whispered on a trembling breath. Since Ennis passed, a despondency so profound literally brought her to her knees in prayer. Speaking to God became the lone thread holding her sanity in tact. For years she pushed Him away, unaware of the comfort He could provide in such difficult situations. Ennis was correct about a lot, she ultimately confessed. He was especially correct about God.

"Excuse me," a voice broke her train of thought. It was Josh Hunter in his department dress blues, and he stepped directly in front of her, blocking her view of Ennis's casket. She strained to see around him, to see her best friend and lover laid to rest. Instead, she felt Josh removing her shield from her uniform, as well as the commendations she'd received over the years. To her stunned expression he plainly said, "You're no longer a police officer so you're not allowed to wear these."

Savannah's mouth worked but her voice didn't. She wondered why now, of all times, he'd chosen to relieve her of her job. Josh, curiously oblivious to her pain, simply explained, "You didn't want them anyway. You told me to keep them, remember?"

She glanced at her uniform, now minus the badge and breast bars. The surreal scene turned even more bizarre when he relieved her of her cap tucked beneath her arm, "Return the uniform by end of day. It's stolen property after that." He smiled, "'Fraid I'll have to arrest you for theft if you don't. I should arrest you for impersonating a police officer since everyone knows you're not much of one in the first place. You should have protected your partner. He would be alive if you'd been a good and loyal cop." Josh stepped back and faded into the mass of people now surrounding the casket.

Even as the first shot rang out from the twenty-one gun salute, she heard a group of people somewhere behind her. They chanted the same phrase and as they neared, the clearer the words became. By the time she looked up, Ennis's brother Cal and his wife Bobbi flanked one side of her while Ennis's other brothers Jake and Dane flanked her other. They all turned to face her saying in unison, "This is your fault. You let Ennis die."

They repeated the words until all in attendance joined them. The thunderous noise quickly grew deafening. Savannah covered her ears in a futile attempt to drown their chants.

The afternoon sun blazed from the sky, seemingly as angry with her as everyone else. The intense heat formed sweat that the breeze didn't cool. She felt blistering hot from the inside out and now a nagging nausea sprouted in her stomach, growing more insistent the warmer she became.

Savannah finally struggled to leave the funeral, pawing

her way through people but they closed around her until she faced the one person she never wanted to. Mama Rutherford. The older woman's face streaked with tears, both hands fisting tissues as she cried, "This is your fault. If only you'd been with him that day..."

When she wheeled away from Mama Rutherford, R.J. appeared and blocked her escape. He glared out of narrowed eyes, "I always told your mama you was the dumbest one of the three. That boy loved you and you wouldn't agree to marry him – not until he was dyin'."

She turned away again, seeking any outlet of freedom from the scrutiny and accusations. This time Jake towered over her, his expression conveying one emotion: rage. She recognized it as the same boiling rage she experienced at the station. "None of us wanted him to move here but he did. Then he met you," he growled, moving closer. "Now he's dead."

His hand seized her throat with such speed and ferocity, it stunned her. His hand was cold as ice on her feverish skin. The fingers bore down until breath was merely a wish. She tore at his steel grip and at last he released her with a mighty shove from his burly, muscular arm and a furious, "You should die too."

Savannah stumbled backward into someone else. It was Dane who said, "He was murdered trying to make you happy." He pointed past her, "He was murdered after buying that for someone who wouldn't marry him."

She looked in the direction his finger pointed. Atop the casket now sat the pink Tiffany's box wrapped in white ribbon. Dane growled, "He bought that for a woman who didn't love him enough to be his wife."

Savannah searched for her sister and brother. Georgia and Seth were nowhere to be found as the crowd converged on her, stating in unison, "This is your fault, this is your fault."

She stepped backward and tripped over what turned out to be Ennis's casket. She tumbled onto the grass that felt hard as concrete, the blades sharp as tiny swords. Merely touching the grass sliced her hands. The sting of bleeding wounds magnified with the heat and irate crowd was too much for her. Family and friends continued their verbal campaign as she backed away on her hands and knees, the grass still slashing her tender flesh. "I loved him!" she cried back at them. "I loved Ennis! It's not my fault! I loved him!"

She tossed a glance over her shoulder to see the honor guard lowering their rifles. When they raised them again they aimed directly at her. Savannah repeated herself until the tears came. She wept uncontrollably, pleading for mercy as the honor guard took aim on her.

The honor guard's aim remained steady, even as one person stepped forward to command them. It was Josh, "You don't deserve mercy, Savannah. It was your job to protect Ennis. You were his partner, you let him down." He raised his hand and the men cocked their rifles.

She stared down the barrels of the dozen rifles trained on her. Confusion reigned in her mind but she knew one thing for sure. "I love Ennis!" she cried from the depths of her soul. "I love him!"

"Savannah," a voice called at the same time the rifles fired. She jerked and whimpered as the voice spoke again, "Savannah, wake up."

She sucked in a deep breath, her wide eyes searching frantically, expecting to see a casket, a mob of people surrounding her and a dozen rifles aimed at her. What she saw was Seth and Georgia bent over her, trying to wake her while Josh, Dane and Mama Rutherford stared on in disbelief. The hospital waiting room seemed mostly vacant except for that group which relieved her somewhat. A few people stared and whispered then turned their attention elsewhere. Savannah didn't care. She tried to catch her breath while wiping the perspiration from her forehead and face. All she wanted to know was, "He's okay, right?" she demanded. "Tell me he's okay."

Georgia smoothed her hair, her brow creased with worry, "Honey, he's fine. He's still in surgery but yes, he's okay."

Seth fell into the seat next to her, "You were having a hell of a nightmare, Van. We'd been trying to wake you for a while."

"I took a pill earlier. Didn't eat with it so I guess it didn't agree with me." She lowered her voice, awkward with the audience staring on, "What did I say while I was out?"

"Couldn't make sense of most of it," he replied. "Just the last part where you said you loved Ennis and screamed 'no'. What the hell was going on?"

Unlike her nightmare, tears came freely in reality as she waved off the question, unable to bring the horror to words and afraid to try even if she could.

7

Savannah heard the voice long before seeing the face. Putting a name with the sharp, piercing tone took no longer than a moment. She remembered the female in question from Texas. It was, without a single doubt, Jenny Lee Crawford, Ennis's high school girlfriend.

Returning from the family's mandated rest period, Savannah still failed to gather the required patience needed to endure Jenny Lee. So far the only good news of the past few days was Ennis's new residence on the fifth floor instead of ICU. His condition remained unchanged, a reality Savannah continued to struggle with. Sleep was a joke and rest evaded her since Ennis's shooting. She'd close her eyes only to be subjected to horrific scenes of him crumpling to the ground or, worse, visions of Ennis dead.

Everyone and everything grated on her now. Instead of sleeping, she showered and researched comas and coma-like conditions on the internet. Savannah didn't care that her eyes were rimmed with dark circles or felt gritty when she blinked. She didn't care that people honked at her when she mistakenly crossed over lanes of traffic while driving to the hospital. She washed down painkillers with half a granola bar and Yoo-Hoo then fought to keep it all down. She felt like utter shit and if Ennis didn't survive, she doubted she would too. So the sound of Jenny Lee Crawford's squawking voice served only to light her temper yet again, only with the intensity of a blowtorch.

Her head couldn't endure an all out battle with the brat from Texas. A brat who treated Ennis like she, upon first sight, personally cultivated him then hand-picked him from the area's Bachelor Patch to be her future husband. A tall, leggy brat with long, raven hair and a figure ending in a set of broad hips measuring at least an axe-handle wide, maybe two. Savannah thought with such brazenly flared hips, Jenny Lee should be required to hang an orange flag from her ass that read "Wide Load". But then Savannah and Jenny Lee shared no love for one another from the day they squared off in Texas when Savannah met Ennis's family. Savannah won that round and intended to win this one too.

She drew a deep, semi-calming breath and instead of barreling into Ennis's room, she wheeled around and marched down the hall. To her surprise, Detective Mathis flagged her down by waving one chubby hand. The rotund cop heaved a few arduous breaths, "You blind and deaf? I've been trying to get your attention ever since the entrance."

Savannah's fingers combed through her hair, "Sorry. I'm just tired."

"You look terrible. Have you had any sleep?"

"When I drift off, I have nightmares. It's not worth it."

"A drink usually helps me when I got trouble sleeping."

Normally, Savannah countered such suggestions with fervent disgust. The one thing never penciled into her life's aspirations was to become a sot like her father. He drank when sleepless, tired, angry, happy or just plain breathing. She served her time with booze and decided to straighten up. Mathis tried to help, she realized that and again shook her head, "I'll pass. I'll sleep when Ennis is better."

"Who's the broad in there with him? She's been there all morning."

The reference to the "broad" triggered another unwelcome homecoming of memories. Ms. Crawford left a path of destruction wider and more thorough than a tornado.

In Savannah's presence, she cranked up the discord until the needle flew off the nuisance scale. Unable to restrain her revulsion any longer, Savannah adapted an overdone Texas accent, "Jenny Lee Crawford of North Texas High School." And with that, destiny gifted her with an additional aggravation: a nervous tic in her right eye. Savannah blinked until finally rubbing at the corner, too exhausted to really get upset.

"What's with the glitzy outfit she's got on?"

Her lip curled as she rubbed her eye. The tic eased into an occasional bother, unlike Jenny Lee who delighted in being the bane of her existence. Lord only knew what the woman threw on before gracing Atlanta with her presence. Savannah remembered the flashy clothes she wore in Texas – skin tight from top to bottom, sequins and all, "She probably mugged Dolly Parton." Her fatigue spoke volumes, "I'm sure she was an annoying cheerleader, judging by her voice."

"Yeah, that does grate on ya after a point," he agreed. He leaned closer, "She's telling everyone she's his girlfriend. I thought you might find it interesting, if not infuriating."

Even on Savannah's own turf, Jenny Lee found ways to peck at her but, as usual, the brassy Texan underestimated her rival, especially her temper, "She's what?"

Mathis stepped back, realizing he'd started a firestorm,

"Whoa, I'm the messenger, remember."

"She's his *high school* girlfriend." From the recesses of her tired mind, a remembrance of Dane came to the forefront. As he and Savannah stood in the Rutherford's pasture watching Jenny Lee blatantly climb on Ennis like a monkey up a tree, Dane cautioned, "If brains were leather, she couldn't saddle a flea but don't underestimate Jenny Lee Crawford. She's out for Ennis like a dog in heat." In those few months, Jenny Lee evidently found courage to declare herself Ennis's fiancée. The courage was probably stuffed somewhere in the expanse of Jenny Lee's jeans, Savannah thought balefully. The audacity alone probably added twenty pounds to her behind.

"Hey, no sweat. Just thought you'd want to know." By that time, a handful of officers gathered upon seeing the two detectives talking. She recognized most from the station. She also recognized apprehension when she saw it. Evidently Miss Jenny Lee paraded around gleefully informing the masses she was Ennis's intended. By their faces, the officers clearly wanted confirmation or a solid denial.

"That," she paused to search for an appropriate yet forthright word, "*female* with Ennis is not his betrothed as she may have led the universe to believe." The venom in her words stung and she didn't really care. Her pleas to God fell on deaf celestial ears, a position she always found herself in. If He listened as Dane nauseatingly reassured, the Man upstairs sure took His sweet time. Ennis slipped into what she considered a coma shortly after his second surgery which, to Savannah, didn't exactly promote faith. Now she had Jenny Lee to contend with. If her life brightened up one more degree, she swore she'd shoot herself.

A whisper among the officers took center stage, "Betrothed?"

Heads swiveled to the confused individual. Savannah recognized him as a young rookie cop still paired with his Field Training Officer. The F.T.O. answered his query with a mild elbow jab, "Fiancée, idiot."

The group nodded at Savannah, all in agreement with her earlier statement. Most shrugged and waved it off, "We knew she was full of shit."

Mathis joined in, "Yeah, she's pretty but once she opens that mouth, it's like being blasted with an air horn."

She forced a chuckle although they all understood the truth of it. Savannah broached the topic that lingered dangerously in her mind for days, "Speaking of joyous subjects, anyone heard news on my career's future?"

All but the rookie dumbly shook their heads. Having

been around Seth's kids, she recognized the expressions as the "not me" look. No one wanted to fess up to information regarding that subject – but they had heard something. Mathis scanned the group then turned his hefty form toward her, "Stop worrying 'bout it. It'll be okay. You just take care of Rutherford." He tilted closer, "And if you get a chance, heave Reba out before she shatters his eardrums."

A tiny smile curved Savannah's lips. She swore Mathis sounded extremely confident about her situation but she knew the truth. Assaulting a suspect in custody – not to mention threatening his life – spelled only one punishment: dismissal from the job. She patted Mathis on the back, "Thanks for your optimism, John. I hope it carries over to Internal Affairs."

Before he had time to respond, another person joined them. "Peach, what're you doin' out here? I figured you'd be in with him."

Most of the officers restrained the urge to display emotion over the cutesy nickname. The rookie couldn't quite manage. He chuckled under his breath only to be jabbed by his F.T.O. again.

Savannah hitched her thumb in the direction of Ennis's room, "He's currently being worshipped by another female at the moment. I thought it rude to interrupt."

Dane screwed his mouth to the side. The quirk reminded her of Ennis. Sometimes it frightened her how alike the two brothers acted. Lately, it saddened her how alike they *looked* also. She kept uttering prayers that Ennis would regain consciousness and be his lively, cheerful self. Tears threatened again and she shored up the determination not to cry.

For his part, Dane grew increasingly curious, "Who is it?"

Mathis answered for her, "His high school girlfriend. She's masquerading as his intended, if you catch my drift."

Dane did, in fact, catch it like a Nolan Ryan fastball and when it hit, he flinched like it hurt, "I'll be right back."

Instinct nagged at Savannah to let him go. Dane's expression described precisely how long Jenny Lee would *not* be staying once he confronted her. Whatever provoked the movement, Savannah didn't know, but her hand touched his arm, stopping him. His dark eyes narrowed at her momentarily though not in a hateful way. As if he read her mind, he asked, "You don't want me to kick her out? She's tellin' everyone she's marrying him, Peach." With each word his temper rose in intensity, "We all know that's a damn lie."

It took every ounce of self control to present it nicely, "She's still his friend."

Savannah felt the waves of heat rolling off him. He hated the idea of leaving Jenny Lee in the room. Actually she'd never seen Dane so mad. His hands clenched then released a couple of times as if he weighed her words against his impulse to toss the interloper out. Savannah saw the latter winning the battle and wrapped her arms around him, "Thank you, Dane."

He hesitated only a moment before returning the embrace. When he did, she felt the tension melt slightly from his body. His tone still shouted his disgruntlement, "I don't know whether you're crazy or too nice for your own good. I'm going in there, Peach, and I'll mind my manners if she does." He held her at arm's length, lecturing, "One wrong move, though, and she's gone."

O   O   O

Not an hour passed when Savannah succumbed to her paranoia. With Ennis unconscious, images of him falling under Jenny Lee's spell taunted her. Jenny was in rare form from what she witnessed earlier. Savannah's limited knowledge of comas hadn't exactly relieved those worries. She'd read personal accounts stating the voices of loved ones helped pull them from their unconsciousness. It was that fact alone that propelled Savannah down the hall, hell bent on making her presence known. Approaching the half-closed door, she paused upon hearing Dane's voice. He sounded none too happy while conversing with Jenny Lee Crawford. Savannah waited and listened.

"They're not engaged." Jenny Lee insisted as cold, hard fact. She reminded Savannah of a dog digging for a bone. No amount of redirecting the animal's attention altered its goal. Jenny Lee backed up her proclamation with, "Jake told me himself it wasn't true." The words surfaced as a dare. Savannah marveled at the woman's audacity. Daring Dane to contradict his brother took guts, considering Dane never hid his aversion for Jenny. If she knew how angry he'd been earlier that hour, the Texan would have packed her bravado and scheduled a flight out that night. And if she realized the total degree of dislike floating around about for her, she'd have chartered a helicopter and departed directly from the hospital.

Savannah clenched her jaw. She wasn't angry at Jake. Knowing him, he failed to understand the depth of Ms. Crawford's obsession with Ennis and felt justified informing her of his and Savannah's not-so-engaged status. It was true then but not now – a fact Jake would soon discover.

"They *are* engaged," Dane emphasized. "He'll tell you

himself when he wakes up. And he'll be none too pleased to see your face hanging over him."

Savannah finally breathed with quiet thanks to Dane. He spoke the words she wanted so desperately to, only his didn't sound bitter like Savannah's would.

A brief silence followed then Jenny Lee squeaked, "You've always hated me, Dane. I don't believe any of your nonsense." Her voice softened and Savannah imagined Jenny Lee leaning over Ennis, kissing him, "When he wakes up, he'll see how much I love him. After all, I came all this way to save him."

Dane fast reached his limit, Savannah sensed it by his ominous tone, "From what? Being deliriously happy? You're treading some thin ice, Jenny Lee. If Savannah saw you now, I'd likely have to tear her off you."

That's my cue. But before Savannah could push open the door, Jenny Lee found a way to slice her to the heart, "This never woulda happened if he'd stayed back home. He coulda worked the ranch with you and the boys." Her voice hardened, "Why he moved here of all places stumps me. And if that woman loves him so much, where was she when this happened?"

Savannah closed her eyes to fight back anger and tears.

Not being with Ennis haunted her day and night. Patrick Dockery would have probably thought twice about shooting at two cops. She and Ennis had each other's backs from Day One. If he hadn't insisted on taking lost time for shopping, she would have been by his side. But he basically ordered Savannah to finish the day's paperwork to allow him preparation time for their anniversary. The decision to follow his instructions never hurt so deeply as it did now.

Dane countered, "Savannah isn't at fault anymore than you are so you'd best crawl off her back."

"That's right," Jenny Lee pouted. "Defend her. Truth is, Ennis knows who loves him most, don't you, honey?"

The thought of Jenny Lee smacking kisses all over Ennis drove Savannah to shove open the door in a vain attempt at cheeriness, "Hi Dane…" Savannah's blue eyes instantly locked on Jenny Lee. The girl from Texas currently resided on the bed, her broad backside half on, half off the mattress and her hand caressing his cheek. Savannah's temper soared. In addition to her bold actions, Jenny Lee's garish attire set her off even more. A sky blue sequined blouse hugged the ample breasts lingering way too close to Ennis's cheek and the white Levis merely framed a perfect target for Savannah's size ten shoes – if she could maneuver her way to Jenny's backside. Every stitch of clothing clung so tight if they burst, Atlanta Medical risked total collapse.

Savannah stewed as Jenny Lee's manicured nails tenderly combed Ennis's hair. She nearly came unglued the instant Jenny's palm cupped his cheek.

It was, at that moment, Savannah realized Dane understood her perfectly. As Jenny Lee placed a kiss on Ennis's lips, Dane stepped between Savannah and the flippant opportunist.

Savannah's jaw ached from clenching. From past experience, Dane knew to brace her shoulders to prevent a surprise attack. He glanced down in her eyes that she knew were glazed with hatred, protectiveness and jealousy. Dane gave her shoulders a gentle squeeze, "Jenny Lee, unless you enjoy being in traction, you'd best leave."

"I'm not goin' anywhere. They ain't engaged 'cause there ain't no ring on that woman's finger. B'sides, he loved me first. First love is always the best."

She bridled every female urge to climb Jenny and start ripping hair out. It seemed Dane envisioned similar goings-on because he told Jenny Lee to shut up. It became clear shutting up was a task she was incapable of, "Don't tell me to hush. Ennis needs a real woman to take care of him. After all, what man wants a police officer for a wife? All men like a female who dresses and acts like a woman. They love the soft curves and lovin' arms of their true love. *And she's not it.*"

Savannah lunged against Dane but with his solid grip, the movement appeared negligible. He cocked an eyebrow in warning and Savannah got the distinct impression the action said "I told you so" and that made her angrier. She didn't want to wear the black hat. She didn't want to be a jealous, possessive woman who directed who did and did not see Ennis, especially when he needed all the support he could get. She fought Dane *and* her gut instinct and allowed Jenny Lee inside, knowing she'd probably cause trouble. Now Savannah paid the price of trying to be kind.

Jenny delighted in digging her claws deeper, "B'sides that, my mama raised a girl who could be a proper wife to a darlin' like Ennis. Her mama didn't raise a girl, she raised a wannabe boy. I'll give Ennis a dozen babies and she won't. Her mama didn't raise her right. "

Savannah gave Dane a monstrous lunge that knocked him backward two steps. No one got away with insulting her mother. She barely coped with Jenny Lee's attacks on her own character but when someone stooped to needling a person's mother... Just the thought pushed her firmly against Dane who tightened his grip so hard the fingertips bore into her flesh. To inform him of her current homicidal mood, Savannah whispered, "If that no-account piranha doesn't vacate the premises and quick, one of us is leaving by way of that window and it won't be me."

"You lay a hand on me," Jenny Lee warned from across the room, "an' I'll file a report on you."

If Dane wouldn't release her, she'd make the best of it, "It's called a complaint, genius, and I don't recall saying I cared what you did." Her career already circled the drain, she was bone tired and hell if punching the bitch didn't make her mouth water. "But if you don't stop wagging your tongue, I'll tie it in a knot and beat you with it."

"Peach, calm down," Dane cautioned, a slight grin brightening his face. Evidently he enjoyed the mental image of her threat. Indeed, the vision of slapping the snot out of Jenny Lee with that gabby flapping tongue warmed her all over too.

Without breaking eye contact with his captive, Dane addressed the interloper, "I'll make a deal with you, Jenny Lee. If you'll take a breather downstairs for an hour, I won't let this wildcat loose on ya. Think real hard before saying no."

Crossing her arms in defiance, Jenny Lee regressed to eight years old, "I'll leave only if she leaves too."

Savannah tensed again causing Dane to reinforce his hold. "You've visited with Ennis today and Savannah hasn't. Fair is fair."

Savannah heard the distinct sound of a kiss. Her brow sank and her lip curled. If Dane held her any tighter he'd leave bruises but, like a lot of things lately, she didn't really care. Unless he held her, there'd be a killin'. Jenny Lee kissed Ennis once more. This time Dane spoke, "He's aware of your feelings, Jenny Lee. Just go."

"Oh, I'll go," she boldly assured, "but I'll be back and there's nothin' she can do about it."

Dane struggled to control Savannah who brazenly challenged his hold, "God sakes, woman," he pleaded. "Get the hell out before I lose my grip on her. You ain't seen a temper till you've seen hers."

No, she hadn't, Savannah grimly reflected. She hated her temper but lately everyone insisted on testing its boundaries. Until Jenny prepared to leave the room, her ignorance remained solid – then she caught a glimpse of Savannah's expression. A distinctive look of fright overwhelmed her, causing her to step not past but *way around* the couple. By the time she approached the door, the swing in Jenny Lee's behind vacated the premises in favor of speed.

8

At precisely the point she thought her life couldn't suck any worse, someone proved her wrong. On this particular day, it was Internal Affairs. The sharks smelled blood and if they looked close enough, they saw her arms flailing and her legs kicking, trying to stay afloat in this turbulent sea called her existence.

For two long hours they questioned, interrogated, insinuated and threatened. For that time she sat, arms folded on the table before her, staring impatiently at her watch. She desperately wished the bums would get to the point and let her go.

Detective Mathis ensured a union delegate represented her considering she'd earlier pledged to endure IA alone. About an hour before the meeting began, Mathis took her aside, whispering, "Don't tell 'em you brought your gun that day."

Confusion temporarily replaced her anxiety. Savannah cut her eyes to the hefty detective, her own tone secretive, "John, a dozen cops saw me that day and if IA catches me in an outright lie –"

"You think too much." He slid his arm around her, drawing her closer, "When I say trust me, trust me, will ya? Tell 'em you came to confront the guy. Hell, tell 'em if you'd *had* your gun, you woulda entertained ventilating the bastard. But whatever you do, don't tell 'em you actually had your gun with you."

With that bit of advice, Savannah's burden doubled. Not only about Internal Affairs but the cryptic suggestion Mathis insisted she take. She sat for a good twenty minutes waiting for her delegate and agonizing over which was worse: telling the truth or a lie.

The entire station house fell deathly quiet as the IA guys, awash in a heavy flavor of outward arrogance, strutted to the interview room. The two dressed like high priced lawyers, one in a gray suit and maroon tie, the other in black with a gray tie. She reconsidered her earlier appraisal. They looked more like mob hit men.

Taking a seat in the interview room, the irony wasn't lost on Savannah. She sat in the same chair as Ennis's shooter when she attacked him. Karma bites back, her brain goaded, and it brandished razor sharp teeth. She was about to lose her job in the same room Dockery nearly lost his life.

In the end, she took John's advice and to the aggravation of her accusers, her delegate spoke more than she had.

The man in charge, Sergeant Wilkins, failed to impress her with his slicked back hair, close-set beady eyes and knife blade nose. A walking weasel, she thought.

Steely also came to mind for him, with glacial a close second. His credibility – and intimidation tactics – waned because a blatant nervous habit of repeating the same question, just with different wording. "The definition of insanity is doing the same thing repeatedly and expecting a different outcome," Albert Einstein once said. Savannah figured the sergeant's manner of asking questions fell into the same category – but she probably wouldn't tell him, at least not on that particular day.

Strangely, she also detected a slight lisp when she frustrated Wilkins. Savannah made it a goal to enhance that lisp to surpass Sylvester the Cat. It succeeded to a point. Mostly it passed the time.

The other man present spoke limitedly, like she. He feverishly took notes similar to a kid attending his first college lecture. His stalwart manner of documenting a person's professional demise seemed clinical, as though he swept over a decade of faithful service out with the garbage. Then the painful truth registered. College Kid didn't do it, *she* did. Savannah mentally shrugged. So what if they dismissed her? If given the chance, she'd have done the same thing a million times over – only she'd have succeeded in killing the bastard who shot Ennis.

After a solid thirty minutes, the sergeant's high-handed attitude and relentless grilling grated her nerves. The barrage of invasive questions first began with rumors of her "personal" relationship with Ennis, the second, her temper. The coup de grace came as no surprise: past reports of borderline conduct with suspects. By that point she stopped counting. Yes, sometimes she smacked a suspect, everyone knew that. A lot of cops did it. Some cops did worse. She stuck to giving certain suspects a wake up call – a slap to the back of their noggins – mainly to show them she knew they were lying.

The questions grew to accusations after an hour. Wilkins evidently assumed the past sixty minutes took a toll and weakened her resolve, or at least her memory of events. He asked unreasonable questions, causing her to swallow the fury growing inside while her delegate spoke for her. She couldn't believe Wilkins actually expected her to spill her guts like she was some shaky, timid rookie facing IA for the first time. He expected her to falter under his scrutiny and melt into a crying heap, probably because of her gender. Little did he know she grew up with a father who detested tears and beat his kids harder for shedding them. Compared to R.J., Wilkins was a schoolyard bully in a suit.

Tears never threatened to surface but her temper certainly did. Her delegate deserved plenty of credit. He countered the unnecessary questions and comments with reserved calm and that, in turn, transferred to Savannah, at least in some remote way.

After her interrogation concluded, she trudged through the station house to see different reactions from her colleagues. Fear resided on the faces of rookies, she assumed because IA was the mythical Big Bad Wolf to all new cops. Several more seasoned cops gave a "thumbs up" as she passed and she acknowledged them with a tired smile. Josh Hunter watched her lumber to the door. When their vision met, his hand raised and he hesitantly waved. She returned the gesture. Then she climbed into her Camaro, drove two blocks and broke down from the stress. It was the first time in years she seriously entertained having a good stiff drink.

Now she sat in the hospital cafeteria head in hands,

staring at three chocolate frosted donuts on a plate. Beside the donuts were a glass of milk and a pint of Jack Daniels. The struggle to push the latter away became monumental. She'd had her day with Jack – years with him, in fact – so when she sobered up, she worked to avoid plummeting into that abyss again. She remembered the warm glow of Jack coating her stomach, easing her troubles. This particular day the bottle's amber brown contents provided a mighty temptation.

She touched the smooth glass. For a moment she wondered if this was how her father felt before leaping into the abyss. Did he balance the consequences of drinking, what it could lead to? Or did he, like she, tell the world to kiss his lily white ass because he was drinking no matter what they did or said?

"A penny for your thoughts or a dollar for your donuts."

Savannah barely heard the voice over the call of the bourbon. When she glanced up, Dane already seated himself across from her, his dark eyes shifting from the bourbon to her weary expression. "Bad day, I take it?"

"My required meeting with Internal Affairs," was all she said.

The gravity of the statement required no further explanation. Savannah was grateful for that. The cafeteria filled quickly with hospital staff and visitors. The clinking and clanking of silverware and coffee cups on trays increased in frequency. A glimpse at her watch revealed the noon hour arrived sooner than she expected. That meant she'd debated about drinking for an hour and a half. After such a time, she also deduced that the cafeteria staff probably labeled her as unstable. On that count, they were correct.

She resumed staring at the bottle then reached for it. From the corner of her eye, she saw Dane flinch as she unscrewed the top and tipped it toward the glass of milk.

If he hesitated, she didn't notice. Dane scooted the milk away, preventing her from spiking it. He said in a low, gentle voice, "Savannah, do me a favor. Hold off on doing this and drink the milk instead."

A spark of temper accentuated a heavy sigh. As though he heard the harsh words flooding her brain, Dane covered her hand and adopted a tone that sounded too much like Ennis, "I'm not telling you what to do. I'm asking you to put that bottle away for now."

Her narrowed vision flicked across the semi-crowded room then centered on her companion, "Give me one good reason. I mean a damn good one." Her tone telegraphed her resentment at his meddling. To Dane's credit his only reaction appeared as pursed lips. She'd kept company with Dane long enough to calculate his next move and before he acted on the clever idea of using Ennis for an excuse, "And don't tell me Ennis wouldn't want me to. He can tell me himself if he comes through this."

His hand squeezed her wrist gently, his compassion deepening. That doubly angered her. All the empathetic looks, uplifting lectures, scriptures from the Bible and God talk drained her. She wanted Ennis back. That was all.

"You haven't given up on him, have you?" he asked.

"Let go of my hand," was the barely restrained command. For Dane Rutherford to ask such a ludicrous question, it practically drove her to unleash the rage building since that morning. Her heart literally ached in her chest each moment Ennis remained unconscious.

Dane obviously sensed the drop in temperature but didn't heed her expression to back off, "I understand your frustration, Savannah. I know you're hurting but you have to give God a chance. He's working –"

"Spare me the God talk, okay? He's still on my list." She carefully enunciated the next few words, "Ennis is still unconscious and frankly I haven't seen a hopeful sign of an impending change." Savannah's temper mounted with each syllable, "No one gives me straight answers about his condition except 'It's in God's hands' and I'll belt the next idiot who says it. I've endured my partner being seriously wounded and have seen him through two critical surgeries. I've battled that twit from Texas and Internal Affairs in the same week. They'll probably kick that asshole loose because of what I did so I can announce to Ennis – if he wakes up – that I single-handedly screwed up the investigation. I'm sure I've lost my job and whether I've lost my best friend is still in limbo then you have the balls to ask if I've given up?"

Dane's mouth opened to respond but she hushed him with a raised hand, "I've given up on plenty in my life but there's one person I'll never give up on and that's Ennis. He's been there for me and I'm there for him." Tears welled in her angered vision, "Don't you ever ask me that again, understand?" It wasn't a question. It left no room for interpretation. It whacked Dane upside the head with the exact amount of weight she intended.

He studied her the way someone gauges how hungry the nearby lion looks, "I apologize." His voice softened, "It's just these type situations test even the strongest folk."

"You're telling me," Savannah grumbled. Sighing, she rested her forehead against her palm in a vain attempt to calm herself. The days grew longer by the second. No amount of distraction eased the tension. She wanted a drink so bad she could almost taste it but Dane wasn't surrendering his hold.

"You're not stopping me from drinking so you might as well let go," she said, matter-of-fact.

Dane fought a response, she could tell. The reply strained against his lips that now paled from pursing so tight but he released her hand. Watching her tilt the bottle toward the milk, he finally muttered, "Wish you'd think twice about it."

With an exhausted grim half-smile, she answered, "I've thought about it more than twice." The bottle tilted over the milk and surprisingly her hand refused to pour the bourbon. It remained at an angle just short of tipping the amber liquid. She saw Dane staring at the bottle, his hands rolled into fists. That helped about as much as her brain seizing up and stopping her hand from pouring. It figured, she complained to herself. Not even her own body cooperated in her misery. She needed relief from this living hell. Sleeping provided none, painkillers worked for a short time but the bourbon would hopefully dull reality a while, or at least it used to.

"There she is," a child broadcasted like she'd found Santa and intended to alert the world. Small shoes pounded the floor and in her peripheral vision Savannah saw Lindsey's dark wavy hair springing about her shoulders as she bounded toward her aunt. Lindsey wasted no time grabbing her in a hug. At this point Savannah knew God existed – and He hated her. He'd done everything short of making a guest appearance to stop her from drinking.

Savannah lifted her weary blue eyes upward, her vision filling with the image of Seth, Georgia and the energized little girl bear-hugging her. The adults focused on the bourbon that she placed back on the table, not a drop dribbled from the pint. Damn.

Returning the hug, Savannah grimaced at the constriction around her neck. Lindsey was into power hugging lately. Each embrace seemed more determined than the last, or maybe Savannah's strength merely waned.

When Lindsey released her, the girl spied the chocolate glazed donuts and licked her lips, "Are you gonna eat those?"

Savannah pushed the plate toward her, "Actually, no. Eat up, kiddo."

The girl piled into the chair beside her, her small hands eagerly swiping a fat donut from the plate. Two bites into it, she pointed to the bourbon, "I want that."

Savannah followed the chocolate covered index finger aiming at the bottle, "Can't have it, sweetheart."

"Why not?" she asked.

"It's not good for you."

She giggled but her aunt found no humor in her current state of affairs. If her niece – and several dozen strangers – weren't present, she'd gladly explain how *not* funny it was. Lindsey licked the chocolate off her fingers, "Then it's not good for you either."

"Lindsey's right," Seth sauntered to Savannah's other side to confiscate the liquor. Savannah swore he gloated, just another thing she seethed over. Everyone tried to run her life. Lindsey's statement fueled Seth to add yet another notch on the sibling's belts. If that wasn't bad enough, Dane joined the triumphant expressions of all those present – except her.

When she slapped a hand on the bottle, the group smile faded. In her nicest tone, Savannah warned, "Leave it alone."

Seth bent to her, his hand bringing her closer by the shoulder as he whispered, "Before we let you start drinking again, Georgia and I will drag your ass to the boondocks and stake it down."

"With or without the anthill nearby?" she asked, her tone remaining even, her grip steadfast on the bourbon. "At last glance I'm thirty years old and in full control of my faculties."

Her brother cleared his throat. The signal wasn't lost on

Savannah who tightly restrained the urge to rise up and slap
him, "Do not throw that incident in my face." Hinting at her
tirade at the station wasn't exactly prudent on Seth's part.
Hiding her anger proved more than she could accomplish and
Dane must have sensed it. He winked at Lindsey and waved
her to him, "Let's get you a big ol' glass of milk to chase those
donuts down."

Lindsey joined him with such ease, it reminded
Savannah of Ennis's rapport with her niece. Something about
the Rutherford brothers just made a girl at home, she supposed.

The instant they were out of listening range, her siblings
converged on her but not before she launched into a subdued
rant herself, "You two back off. I've had a shitty day because I
met with Internal Affairs. Either of you want my life, take it,
but once you have it, keep it. Don't temporarily adopt it, gnarl
it up then hand it back. Until you're in my skin, don't march in
and try to commandeer my life."

Seth planted himself next to her, "We're trying to help.
You've already pulled one foolish stunt, don't add to it by
drinking."

Savannah's vision played across the room. More hospital
staff and visitors sat down to their meals, congregating in small
clusters, minding their own business. A constant hum of voices

filled the immediate area which aided in containing the outburst perched on her tongue. The blood rushed to her face, her hands fisted. A touch on her shoulder barely registered. Georgia's soft tone finally broke through, "We both know Seth sucks at diplomacy."

Savannah trained her vision on her brother. "Sucks" barely scratched the surface. If the country elected him President, he'd make short work of destroying any alliances the U.S. might have. She didn't doubt that the allies themselves would probably heave a couple of nukes in response to something he'd said.

Georgia gestured to Seth who sighed his annoyance but resigned his current position, allowing her to take his place. The older sister tried her hand at conversing, "Honey, don't resort to this again. It didn't work then, it won't work now. What is your normal routine when you're stressed?"

Georgia knew the answer but evidently wanted to make a point. "I run," was the simple response. She followed it with, "But it's impossible when Ennis is still in trouble. I'm concentrating on him right now."

"It would help to run off some stress. Ennis won't be alone. We'll be here and Mama will be too –"

"That's not the point, Georgia. I want to be with him."

Lindsey and Dane returned with not one glass of milk but two. Dane carried the regular whole milk while the girl sat a glass of chocolate milk on the table. She scooted it toward her aunt, "Dane said it's the next best thing to a Yoo-Hoo."

Savannah stole a peek at Dane. His dark brow lifted as if asking her to try it. She couldn't exactly lose her cool at the gesture. It didn't ease the craving for the bourbon but it stopped her from outright saying no. She realized everyone waited, even Lindsey. The girl nudged it closer then covertly whispered, "It's good. Dane got me some but I already drank it."

Savannah smiled despite herself. She leaned down, whispering back, "If you say it's good, I'll drink it." She thought she heard a group sigh when she opted for the chocolate milk. The tension in Dane's features eased, and she felt a reassuring hand on her shoulder. It was Georgia.

With that, Lindsey changed conversational gears once more, "Mama says Aurora's gonna have babies."

Aurora was another fish in Lindsey's collection. It was a black and white bubble eye goldfish. Somehow Savannah sensed another gift being offered. She wasn't wrong. "You and Uncle Ennis can have one."

Savannah appreciated the thought, she really did, but if

she wasn't careful her house would rival the Georgia Aquarium. Seth's children amazed her. Between Lindsey and her younger brother Dylan, Savannah and Ennis now owned three Dr. Seuss books, two fish and six crayon drawings, the latter illustrating their impending wedding. Savannah only wished she was as thin as Dylan depicted her. She was thankful Ennis's nose was considerably shorter than her nephew's image of it. Her sweetheart resembled a baby woodpecker. The drawings hung on the refrigerator, the books sat on her entry table, and the two fish currently resided in a goldfish bowl with the price tag still stuck on the side. She loved her niece and nephew but another fish, she was quite certain, wasn't the answer. "Thank you, sweetheart, but Uncle Ennis and I are partial to Faith and Hope. We don't want to crowd them."

Lindsey already plowed into the second donut, her mouth half full as she spoke, "Then you'll have three different colors of fish!"

"Yeah," Seth joined in to Savannah's disgust, "what's Faith and Hope without Charity?"

She smiled a tense smile at Seth, "Ut-shay, up-ay."

Lindsey giggled, "Aunt Savannah told Daddy to shut up. Daddy doesn't like that, even when Mama says it."

Seth bent closer, saying in a low tone, "That's because

Mama says it so often."

The declaration nearly made Savannah smile. She figured her brother caused quite a fuss at times. Leah, like most women, tolerated only so much until ultimately losing their composure.

A vibration on her hip forced her attention to her cell phone. Savannah opened it and stared at the name, "Here's the icing on today's cake," she announced to no one in particular. She answered the phone to hear her boss's voice, "How'd it go with IA?"

"Besides dousing me in kerosene and teasing me with lit matches, it went okay." Her description halted any discussions in her immediate surroundings. Her family stared with wide eyes except Lindsey who'd busied herself eating the remainder of the donuts.

"Hang in there," Josh encouraged. "They've still got plenty of interviews to go, even mine. I'll do what I can."

"Thanks," she replied. She meant it too. The more she thought about losing her job, the deeper she descended into depression. That and Ennis's situation tapped her out mentally and physically.

He cautiously slid into the subject of his call, "I do have some bad news though."

"What a surprise," she sighed. "Well, lay it on me."

"There's talk of kicking Dockery loose."

Before she could control it, the word sprang boisterously from her lips, "What?"

Conversations a few tables away now ceased. Savannah felt weak and enraged all at once but she'd spent so much adrenaline lately, the weakness won out. Truthfully, she expected it. She forewarned Dane about it and thought she halfway prepared herself. Apparently, she failed. To hide the anger and tears, she leaned her forehead into her palm, "Did the D.A. find out?"

"Not yet, at least I don't think so. Savannah, don't go ballistic. It's a maybe, not a for sure. I just wanted you to know."

"There's a reason they're thinking of cutting him loose and I want to know why."

Josh paused a good five seconds, "I think Connelly muddied the water. He may have said something to IA to raise their interest. He's been quiet all day and no one'll have anything to do with him."

Judging by Josh's choice of words, Connelly muddied the water to the consistency of the Mississippi River. When the squad shunned a cop, they had a reason. She tried to place the rookie Connelly in the confusion of the scuffle. He wasn't the rookie on guard duty at the interview rooms. Even as her mind replayed the event in slow motion, she never located him in the throng of blue uniforms. "Was he there?"

"According to the duty roster, yes. He was supposed to be filling out paperwork but no one remembers seeing him at the time, not even his training officer. I'll talk with him and his F.T.O. later and get to the bottom of it."

"Thanks. I appreciate it."

"Anytime. Keep a good thought and tell Ennis we're praying for him."

"Will do," she clicked off and clipped the phone to her belt. She glanced up to see anticipation written heavily in her family's expressions. No one dared speak except Lindsey, "Who was that?"

"My boss. He's trying to save me from getting a job as a dogcatcher."

Lindsey giggled and again, Savannah lacked the fortitude to join in. The thread holding her universe together continued the torturous process of unraveling. She eyed the bourbon through narrowed vision, debating over swilling it down. The decision appeared quickly – save it for later when she wouldn't just crave it, she'd beg for it.

"What'd he say?" her niece inquired as Seth reached across with a napkin. He motioned to the corners of her mouth. Lindsey took the hint and wiped the chocolate away.

"He said to keep a good thought."

"What else?" Dane inquired.

"IA's threatening to cut Dockery loose. Josh doesn't know exactly why except one rookie might have suffered diarrhea of the mouth."

On that note, Lindsey's lip curled, "Yuck, Aunt Savannah. That's nasty."

"Yes, it is, sweetheart," she agreed, settling for another healthy swallow of the creamy chocolate milk. "And it might get nastier as time goes on."

O O O

Instead of drinking the bourbon, she headed for home. She needed time to sort things out in the quiet of home where things seemed safe, stable. While gathering more reading material for Ennis, she found herself staring into her closet, wondering if she should disturb a different kind of reading material. This particular item required digging for. It sat in a box on the top shelf of her closet, untouched for over ten years. After acquiring a stool, she retrieved the box, carefully dusted it off then opened it. The leather bound book remained in pristine condition, just like that day her mother presented it to her. In the lower right corner in gold script read, "Savannah Prince".

Without removing it from the box, Savannah folded back the cover, opening the book to the dedication page. In bold black lettering were the words "This Bible is presented to" then in Charlene's handwriting read, "My darling little girl. May the words within always provide comfort and hope."

Her mother entered her thoughts more lately than ever. Charlene's faith never wavered, even facing death. Savannah found her devotion incredible. Through the beatings R.J. subjected her to, through the loss of many close relatives to her own impending death, Charlene held strong to the Bible, to God.

Savannah stroked the cover and strangely felt her mother's presence. Now she lifted the book from the box and opened it. Her mother bookmarked specific pages when presenting it to her. Savannah turned the pages to a burgundy satin bookmark. Reading silently at first, she found herself speaking the words aloud, "If ye have faith as a grain of mustard seed, ye shall say unto this mountain, Remove hence to yonder place; and it shall remove; and nothing shall be impossible unto you."

Another bookmark was handwritten by her mother, "With God, all things are possible," it said. Savannah wiped the growing tears filling her eyes. "Then why did He take you from me? I really need you now and He robbed me of your guidance and love." She wanted to close the book and never open it again. She wanted to forget she ever opened it since it forced her to revisit the pain she felt when her mother died. But something held her hands steady, the Bible open.

She swiped another tear with the back of her hand, looked down and read a highlighted passage, a passage Charlene wanted her to see so many years before. Savannah read it for the first time, "I sought the Lord, and He heard me, and delivered me from all my fears." She noted the book was Psalms. Another marked passage in Psalms read, "In God have I put my trust: I will not be afraid what man can do unto me."

With every verse Charlene bookmarked, Savannah found herself wanting to read more. In a way, it was like visiting her mother again. She remembered going to church, singing the hymns and being so happy when her mother smiled down at her. At that age, the pride in her mother's expression encouraged her to attend church and read the Bible. Somehow the feeling dwindled over the years. She wondered if Charlene would still be proud of her. Yes, in some ways, her intuition said. In others, she'd be disappointed, particularly about her choice to ignore God.

Thumbing through her Bible, Savannah ran across a folded piece of paper, again in Psalms. Unfolding it, she realized her mother left a note inside the book that she'd never read. "My little girl, I want you to let God lead you during the difficult times. If you feel lonely, call on God. I worry about you since you're more independent than Georgia or Seth. I'm afraid you'll try to shoulder all your burdens without the love of the Lord to help. Please trust God. He will not abandon you."

Her tears flowed freely now. She set aside the Bible and note and buried her face in her hands, giving in to the emotion. Her mother knew more than she expected. She knew Savannah's faith would not only stumble during hard times, but she would fall when it happened.

"Oh, Mama, I miss you so much," she cried. "I want to hear you and see you again. I want you to hold me and tell me Ennis will be okay. I want you back."

She cried until tears couldn't fall anymore. The crying wrung her out until a bone weary exhaustion overwhelmed her. She was so tired of fighting, so tired of bearing the weight of her worries. She wanted Ennis back, and with that would come peace and happiness again. Agonizing over his condition took more strength than she imagined or possessed. She needed help coping, help that no human could provide. Help that no drink could supply.

The note still lay open on the bed as did the Bible. At the bottom of the note Charlene wrote a verse from Isaiah, "Fear thou not; for I am with thee: be not dismayed; for I am thy God: I will strengthen thee; yea, I will help thee; yea, I will uphold thee with the right hand of my righteousness."

She folded the note again, placed it in the exact spot she found it and closed the Bible, held it to her heart. "It's hard for me, Mama. To put my trust in God again. But if He provided you the comfort and love to see you through the hard times, I'll turn to Him too..."

9

Something warm and soft brushed Ennis's forearm. The touch went from his elbow down to clasp his hand. Without opening his eyes, he knew Savannah's touch from memory. Her gentle caresses were emblazoned in his mind, along with her beautiful face and sultry voice. Out of a thousand women, recognizing her would be a cinch. He could find her blindfolded by her unique essence of lavender. The delicate fragrance of her perfume now wafted into his nostrils, bringing his senses alive and him from the depths of slumber.

Where his senses functioned fine, his memory refused to cooperate in some respects. His primary question – why did he currently reside in a hospital? He'd heard nurses fussing over him, doctors giving instructions about him and, most of all, he heard Savannah worry over him. For what seemed his life's entirety he'd fought his way back to her, to his one and only.

The struggle drained him, badgered at him to give up but he trudged through the dense forest of pain and now was rewarded with the feel of Savannah's kiss on his forehead.

Her voice remained his anchor throughout his unconscious period. From the abyss of nothingness, he heard her speaking to him, reading to him, telling him jokes and anecdotes of her life. She told him her dreams about their honeymoon and their life together. She'd read endlessly from Zane Grey's "Riders of the Purple Sage", one of his favorites. When she switched to telling jokes, one in particular remained in his mind. "Here's a new one from Lindsey," she had said. "What did the letter say to the stamp?" Ennis recalled the joke from childhood as, no doubt, Savannah did too. What he couldn't recall was the punch line. "Stick with me and we'll go places," she finished. He'd heard the smile in her tired voice. He loved to see her smile...

Her soft lips now brushed his knuckles as he heard her whisper, "God, let him come back to me. I pray you'll bring him back." Even in his post-surgery fog, the prayer caught him by surprise. Savannah never claimed to be religious. In fact, since he'd known her, she'd always dismissed the fact God was there or that He listened. She'd explained why, because of her childhood and later, her mother's death, she'd given up on believing. To hear Savannah pray for him nearly shocked him back into unconsciousness.

Now that he lingered in a semi-conscious state, he noticed Savannah's hands trembled as they held his, contrary to the steady hold he was accustomed to. A velvet stroke complemented her hold, telling him she swept her cheek across his knuckles. Ennis willed himself to respond, told his finger to caress her cheek while in her hold. He'd missed her so intensely his soul ached and he yearned to show her he was back, that they were together again.

He rallied every muscle possible to follow directions. *Brush her cheek*, he instructed his fingers. *Brush against her and she'll know...* At first he was unsure anything happened then he felt her stiffen slightly, the hold on his hand tighten. Then Ennis felt a trembling smile against his fingers and followed closely by Savannah's hopeful voice, "Ennis, are you awake? Please be awake."

He swore his eyes were glued shut. No matter how he struggled, the lids refused to lift. Savannah's lips pressed kisses to his knuckles, encouraging him. He wanted to see his sweetheart so badly. It seemed like years since they'd embraced or kissed. He remembered going to surgery with a thrill of excitement rolling through him. Had she said she'd marry him or had he merely dreamed it? Bracing her now with it was hardly prudent – what if he'd imagined it? Then he would feel snake belly low asking her for clarification.

Ennis made an attempt to clear his throat which proved to be a mistake altogether. His throat hurt like a bitch, the rawness even traveled as far down as his toes. His effort, however, brought Savannah closer and she smoothed his hair, "I'm right here, babe. You don't have to talk, just squeeze my hand."

He did squeeze her hand but he begged to differ with her. He did need to talk but the way his throat burned, verbalizing his feelings would have to wait. Instead, when she grasped his hand a bit tighter, he returned the gesture then slackened his hold. The action basically panicked her, "Is something wrong? Squeeze my hand if you need a nurse."

Ennis pushed himself to open his hand and willed his fingers to shift around hers. His fingers gradually moved, grazing her soft skin. She'd been holding his hand in her left one and he longed to make his point before she caused a riot among the nurses. Savannah's voice developed a panicked quality, her words came fast, much too fast for him to keep up. He focused on his goal, not her anxiety, and mentally counted – index, naughty then ring finger. Fatigue settled in fast, his hand slowed its movement as the acute weariness threatened to sweep over him. Ultimately, he found his treasure and curled his hand around the third finger of her left hand. The act, a monumental accomplishment for him, finally shushed her.

The stress drained from her hold, the trembling finally settled. Relief washed over Ennis when he heard her voice return to the normal low, sultry tone, "Oh, *that's* what you're trying to say." She stroked his forearm long and slow as she pressed his hand to her heart, "Honey, I'll marry you but first you have to get better, that's the only catch to it."

In his mind he beamed like a kid at Christmas. Inside, his soul danced. Then he fell asleep.

10

It started as a simple trip home to feed Faith and Hope. Lindsey not only gifted them but named them as well – with a generous amount of help from her parents, Savannah suspected. Seth explained the names were reminders that no one should forsake faith or give up hope. Nothing like children (or their parents) to put a guilt trip on a person, Savannah thought.

The gift came at an inopportune time with Ennis still in the hospital but Savannah realized Lindsey wanted to help. Giving the fish was her way of saying "everything will be okay".

Savannah still doubted a third would fit comfortably in the bowl but Lindsey insisted on presenting them with Charity whenever Aurora's offspring arrived. Savannah spent a few minutes watching the happy little orange and white bubble eye goldfish swim. They wiggled back and forth upon sight of her like they welcomed her home. She imagined the reception rested in their hunger, not their joy of seeing her.

She'd rushed home long enough to sprinkle some food in their bowl since Faith and Hope couldn't possibly survive on the basis of their names. They swam energetically toward the flakes drifting down in the water, her presence long forgotten. After taking a moment to grab a Yoo-Hoo and check the answering machine, she hit the road to the hospital.

By the time she trudged back into Atlanta Medical, an hour passed which turned out to be long enough for a nuclear meltdown to occur in her absence.

Her feet long since memorized the trail to Ennis's room. Exhaustion wore so heavily, not even her claustrophobia kept her from riding the elevator instead of climbing the stairs. Once Ennis showed signs of consciousness, her brain and body conspired to collapse. For days she ran on adrenaline, now she felt physically wrung out and wilted. Emotionally, she felt like a lottery winner – and she won the biggest jackpot ever.

The elevator ride seemed longer that day so she leaned against the wall for a respite. The doors finally opened and her feet took over from there, walking past the waiting room where she waved at Mama and Georgia who appeared to be in paradise playing with Lindsey and Dylan.

Savannah's feet led the way down the long quiet hall, her brain counting doors until both brain and feet concluded they stood at Ennis's door. She confirmed her location by glancing at the name plate posted outside the room. "Rutherford, E." it said. This, indeed, was the place.

She pushed the door open, turned and shut it behind her. Just as the latch clicked into place, a woman's voice greeted her, "Hello, Savannah."

Savannah's eyes closed and her shoulders slumped at the mere sound of Jenny Lee. To the detective, the raucous female amounted to a pesky parasite, sucking the life out of even the strongest humans. What struck her as odd was the manner of Jenny Lee's salutation. She'd never addressed her as Savannah – ever. Since the first introduction in Texas, Jenny Lee labeled her as "that woman" or simply "her". Why the change today?

Unhurriedly rotating on her heel, Savannah rubbed her forehead to rid herself of the growing pang, "Hello, Jenny Lee."

"I'm glad to see you."

Now she knew something was wrong. For that twit to be glad to see her was foreign for Jenny Lee Crawford. Savannah steeled herself to whatever trick or barb awaited her. She risked opening her eyes since she never put anything past a jealous woman. Jenny could have been leveling a hatchet at her skull for all she knew. Best to be ready to run or react in some way...

Her tired blue eyes scanned for signs of danger then settled on Jenny's posture. She sat in the chair, elbows propped on the bed near Ennis's hip, his hand in hers. That alone stoked a flame of anger but only temporarily. What her vision migrated to next blew her away. Seated on Jenny Lee's left ring finger was a small, one stone diamond engagement ring.

Savannah's reaction stunned even herself. Instead of launching herself at the black haired witch, she merely sighed. A distinct dizziness rolled through her brain forcing her to lean against the door. She concluded Jenny Lee's nefarious brain worked overtime concocting scenarios and lies that tempted even the likes of Job to assault the bitch. Evil dwelled in the Texan's psyche, yanking virtuous ideas and replanting them with menacing thoughts. At her worst, Jenny never stooped to this degree of lying about hers and Ennis's relationship. But, Savannah reminded herself, ugly surprises sprang from every corner with the woman.

Even as Savannah's instinct warned her to calm down, the sight of the ring *and* Jenny Lee physically cozying up to Ennis wore on already frayed nerves.

"Are you okay, sweetie?" Jenny pouted with a mischievous twinkle in her eyes.

The door pushed against Savannah's back once then twice. She didn't trust herself to move. Visions of sequins littering the floor as Savannah shouldered Jenny Lee through the small window warmed her like an addict getting a long awaited fix. Soon, she feared, the images' cathartic effect would wear off, provoking her to truly act on the fantasy. That damn ring on Jenny Lee's finger had to be a hoax. The gleaming little rock shimmered at her, goading her to fly mad.

The door gave a solid shove against her back, forcing her forward a few steps.

"Were you standing there, Peach?" Dane offered a quick apology for barging in, "We thought the door was stuck." He glanced from Savannah to Jenny Lee and his expression darkened, "Oh, hell."

Georgia followed Dane inside, her attention focused more on Savannah than Jenny. Dane stalked toward the latter, "Let's go, Jenny Lee. I'm not going through this again. My muscles ache from all these confrontations you two have."

Georgia tilted her head to study Savannah's expression, "Honey, what's wrong?"

Savannah swallowed dryly, her tongue locked in idle to ensure no foul words emerged. Staring at the taunting engagement ring made her ill but, like a train wreck, she couldn't look away.

"You can't throw me out, Dane Rutherford," Jenny countered, cuddling closer to Ennis. "Ennis and I are engaged to be married. Here's my proof."

Georgia gasped as if someone announced Elvis was alive and standing right behind her. The older sister now angled for a view around Dane to see the "proof". Savannah knew the exact moment she spied it because Georgia took her hand and began a campaign of pep talks that rolled off the younger Prince like water off a duck's back. The engagement was a blatant lie, she realized that and Georgia needn't have worried. Instead, she should have concerned herself with removing the garish Texan from the premises.

The sight of the ring incited Dane's temper as well, "You're some piece of work, Jenny Lee. Ennis didn't propose to you."

The two sisters watched Jenny Lee's anger boil over at Ennis's brother, "Yes, he did. He put this very ring on my finger and proposed marriage to *me*, not her."

Savannah finally found her voice and attempted to bury the fib once and for all, "You mean he just woke up and proposed in the last hour?" The consequences of her question were a violent eruption none of them prepared for.

Jenny Lee rose, hands fisted and stomped toward Savannah. "I'm tired of defending myself to you. Truth is, Ennis and I grew up together and he did propose to me. I don't care who believes me." Jenny aimed a perfectly manicured index finger at her, "Especially you. Ennis and I are getting married. Cope with it, bitch."

Georgia wrapped an arm around her sister before the harsh words registered with her temper, "Dane, we're taking a walk."

"Good idea," he spoke without moving his vision from Jenny. He did, however, move in front of her to block her path, "Jenny and I need to talk."

o o o

Dane purposefully slid his hands in his pockets for fear he'd smack a woman for the first time in his life. Jenny Lee deserved it, no doubt, but he refused to shame his mama. She raised her boys to respect women and, at the very least, tolerate the difficult ones. Both Jenny Lee and Savannah were difficult but for two different reasons. When Savannah showed that side, she protected someone she loved. When Jenny displayed her bad side, it was for Jenny Lee's benefit only. With half the explosive pair removed from the room, Dane felt confident bloodshed could be avoided. "Where'd you get the ring? The downtown Kmart?"

Jenny crossed her arms, "Ennis gave it to me."

Dane's blood pressure rose and he balled his fists that still stayed safely in his jeans. "My brother doesn't make a habit of proposing to just any woman."

She moved back to Ennis's side and tenderly smoothed his hair, "Dane, you're upsettin' him with all this talk."

"He's not nearly as upset as he'll be when you tell him *you're* his bride to be."

Jenny scowled at Dane, "Okay, Mr. Know It All. If I'm lyin' why does he keep sayin' my name instead of hers?"

Dane wondered if she'd slipped a cog. Firstly, Ennis wasn't capable of speaking articulately or clearly at the current time. They were all just joyous when his lips moved at all. Which, once he glanced at his brother, he saw that very thing happening. Ennis's features, however, showed discontent or pain. Jenny Lee suddenly took a back seat to Dane's worries, "Ennis, is something wrong?"

Jenny Lee's long fingers combed Ennis's hair, but only further irritated him and Dane. The latter called her off a moment while he leaned to listen closer. Ennis struggled to speak, his eyes squeezed shut, his lips moving shakily and his words indistinguishable. Dane touched his shoulder, "Calm down, brother." He repeated the words until Ennis settled in, his face beginning to relax, his lips moving slower. Dane leaned closer again, urging him to try once more. He relied on his hearing more than sight to understand his younger brother. Ennis reiterated his previous ramblings only this time Dane caught important syllables and emphasis. A smile split his face, "Loud and clear, bro."

"What is it?" Jenny Lee wanted to know. "Is he okay?"

Straightening, he patted Ennis's shoulder. "Jenny Lee, what exactly do you think he's saying?"

Affronted by his obvious skepticism, she plopped her hands on her hips, "I *know* he's sayin' my name plain as day."

"Then you need to listen closer. Before I tell you the truth, I want to know about the ring."

"He did propose." She crossed her arms, her tone verging on hurt, "He gave it to me two months after graduation."

"Graduation? That's nine years ago, for cryin' out loud."

"Don't say it like that. I love Ennis –"

"Then why ain't you married and got two or three rug rats already?"

She huffed her way to the chair and plunked down in it, "'Cause I thought I loved someone else. I turned Ennis down and kept the ring. When he came home at Thanksgiving last year and he was still single, I thought we might still have a chance." The next few words dripped heavy with venom, "Until she showed up."

Dane's left eye twitched. His hands threatened to haul off and slap the woman within an inch of her life. He'd always known she was a fraud and a user. Good thing she turned Ennis down all those years ago or he'd be living a life of utter hell.

"What do you think he's sayin'?" she finally asked.

Dane rarely found such pleasure in life. An opportunity as singularly perfect as this came forth but once in a blue moon, as his mama would say. It gave him great joy to inform Jenny Lee, but he stood back in case she started swinging...

O O O

Savannah tried to obey her sister, to leave Dane talking with Jenny Lee. The longer they walked the halls, the madder she grew until she blurted an apology to Georgia then sprinted back to the elevator.

Why should she be separated from Ennis when Jenny Lee repeatedly proved her intention – to break them up. Savannah trusted Dane to protect hers and Ennis's relationship. Point was, she hated leaving the entire job to him.

She approached the door once again. The silence inside worried her. Had the two launched into a wrestling match and been removed? It took one second to dismiss the theory. Dane's raising prevented him from handling women in a harsh manner. More than likely, he convinced Jenny to leave peacefully for the time being.

She listened at the door again, and hearing nothing, proceeded to open it. Suddenly it flung open, allowing a veritable storm to sweep past. The black-haired whirlwind sobbed and blubbered by her but not before knocking her backward a few steps. *That does it*, Savannah's weary brain concluded. She clenched her fists as Jenny Lee Crawford blindly raced down the hall, leaving a shower of tears in her wake. Just as Savannah started forward another tornado bulled its way out of Ennis's room and accidentally knocked her back again. This time, though, an apology was offered, "Sorry, Peach. You okay?"

"I'm fine," she answered, her temper receding at Dane's concern. She hitched her thumb down the hall, "What's her problem?"

Dane adopted a smug grin, "Well, you know us Rutherford boys. If there's a way to pitch a monkey wrench into the works, we won't throw it, we catapult it."

Assuming Dane verbally paved the road for Jenny's departure, Savannah gratefully embraced him, "Thank you, Dane. Besides Ennis, you're the most endearing rascal I know."

He gave her a strong embrace in return, teasing, "Don't go sayin' that too loud. First, you'll give people the wrong idea about big bad me. Second, it's kinda like tellin' a man he's cute when he's naked. Much as I'd love to take credit, I didn't toss Jenny out."

They parted the embrace in time for her brow to sink, "Then what was the drama queen show just now?"

Dane lips lifted into a grin, "*I* didn't do it, Ennis did."

"He's awake?" Impulse drove her to the door, not caring a hoot anymore about Jenny Lee. She wanted to talk to Ennis and hear his voice. She yearned to finally see those handsome brown eyes once again.

Dane stopped her with one hand, his other making a so-so motion, "Not exactly awake yet but he's getting there. Still not opening his eyes and his speech isn't all that clear sometimes."

Her heart sank followed closely by her stomach. The excitement built so suddenly that the disappointment was evident in her posture, "Then how did he toss her out?"

Smugness replaced the sheepish grin, "He called her 'Savannah'. That one was unmistakable. Clear as crystal he said your name."

With that news, her slumping shoulders lifted and her face brightened into a thoroughly blissful smile. She felt sort of bad for Jenny Lee but not so much that it kept her from racing inside with hopes Ennis was still awake. She kissed him, called his name and prayed to God for him to respond.

A few moments of silence followed. Savannah felt her heart sinking again, even as she lifted his hand in hers. She'd missed one of the only times Ennis was conscious. She was busy cursing herself inwardly when his lips moved. He struggled to speak but, as Dane said, it was unmistakable, "Savannah."

Thrilled that he was awake, she kissed him, "I'm right here, babe."

He remained still, so still that she feared he drifted away again. But surprisingly, he whispered certain words slowly and methodically, "Letter... say... to... stamp?"

Tears filled her vision and spilled down her cheeks. God

heard her prayers. He brought Ennis back to her. She held Ennis's hand to her lips and kissed it softly. Her sweetheart had returned and he remembered one of the jokes she'd told. What did the letter say to the stamp? A genuine smile brightened her features, "Stick with me and we'll go places."

11

After another day, Ennis's ability to coherently converse improved somewhat. His head slowly cleared, the fog parted to a degree when moments of clarity hit him, they hit hard. One subject continually plagued him and upon opening his eyes, the feeling grew in intensity like an uncontrolled wildfire. His vision always came to rest on Savannah which helped ease the nagging sensation but also strengthened it.

Since the beginning, without fail, he sensed Savannah's presence by his side. As he regained consciousness, he noticed his every move brought her wide awake and to her feet. His hearing grew more attuned as his body slowly recovered from its trauma and surgery. He heard the anxiousness in her voice, felt it in her hold. So when his hand shifted on the blanket, it was no surprise she was on her feet immediately.

"Savannah," his voice rasped a subdued whisper. Warm, velvet lips pressed to his forehead with a tenderness that nearly lulled him back to sleep. "What is it, baby?" she replied as softly as her kiss. Ennis loved her voice, the sultry pitch seasoned with a light Georgia accent made him fall in love all over again.

"I love you." He ceaselessly struggled to speak the words aloud. He fought the drugs and his condition to express his affection for her. Loving someone so deeply literally hurt on occasion. The anguish of separation left his heart lonely and aching.

When Savannah spoke, he heard a smile in her voice, "I love you too, sweetheart. I love you so much."

The same nagging reared itself once more. His brain reminded him now that he was awake, he really *needed* to broach the subject. He'd left two things in his truck. Two *very* important things. After a dry swallow, he maneuvered his tongue to form the correct words, "My truck."

He heard her smile grow, "Don't worry about your truck," she assured. "Dane drove it to our place. It's safe and sound."

Ennis struggled to open his eyes but put most of his

effort into speaking. "Inside. It's inside the truck."

She stroked his hand then his arm, "Are you talking about my anniversary gift? It's safe too. Officer Meade gave it to me like you asked him."

He wanted to tell her but at the same time he didn't. The drugs may have made him loopy, but they didn't make him stupid. "There's something else. Where's Dane?"

The warmth of her hand disappeared as she carefully laid his on the bed, "I'll go get him." She kissed him again which, now that he felt more awake, made him want more. He hoped asking for his brother hadn't hurt her. Maybe she would understand later.

What seemed an eternity passed before his brother stood at his side, "Whatcha need, bro?"

Ennis fought his eyelids and finally popped them open. With monumental effort, he crooked his finger at his brother, waving him closer in case Savannah lingered outside the door, "Her ring is in my truck. Glove box. Get it, bring it. Please."

Dane's eyes widened, "You're taking this marriage thing kinda fast aren't you? Get out of here first then propose."

"No," he intended to say it louder. Dane failed to realize how desperate he was. For a year and a half he labored to change her mind about marriage. Now that he had her, he refused to let her change it back. "Bring it now," he croaked. The effort caused a hard coughing spasm to rip through him and his hand touched close to the wound. His whole chest throbbed when he coughed and he bit back a cry in favor of a spirited groan.

Savannah poked her head inside the room, making Ennis grateful he'd whispered earlier. He nodded slightly and tried for a big smile to show he was fine. He felt like shit though and if Dane didn't follow his instructions, he would about the same.

The degree of concern etched into his love's face firmed his resolve. "Please, Dane."

Dane glanced over his shoulder to see the worry in Savannah's expression. She finally asked if something was wrong. The elder Rutherford shrugged it off, "Nah, he's already making demands. I'm tellin' ya, Peach. You're signin' yourself up for quite a ride with him. He'll be forever insisting you do this and do that. He's impossible."

Ennis tried his best to swat at Dane but it came across limp and lame. For the first time during a conscious moment he brought his hand to his face and rubbed his jaw. A fair amount of confusion wrinkled his brow. Savannah saw it, "Ennis, what's wrong?"

"Somebody been shaving me?" He couldn't believe the

smooth skin beneath his touch and he knew damn well he should have been bushy by now.

Dane hitched his thumb to Savannah, "I wouldn't do it. I figured you'd slap me."

Ennis drew his palm down his cheek again and one brow arched, impressed. He tried his hand at a sly expression, "You been bathing me too, you minx?"

To his disappointment, she shook her head, "I wasn't that confident considering you're attached to a few things under your blanket. Don't worry, I'll make up for it later."

"It's a date."

"Oh, get a room," Dane complained good-naturedly. "Or wait for the honeymoon, either one."

Savannah winked then bowed out of the room, leaving Ennis and Dane alone again. Ennis shifted his tired vision to his brother, "I'd ask Ma to get the ring but Savannah will suspect something."

A robust laugh burst from his brother's lips, "You do remember how this transpired, right? Savannah agreed to marry you so it doesn't matter if she suspects anything."

Ennis puffed up despite the cloud of medication. How could he convey the importance of his request? "It matters to me," he sternly emphasized. Clearly he expressed his fortitude because Dane backed off a step, a smile still brightening his features, "Okay, don't get riled. Your fiancée will kill me and after what I've seen, I truly believe she could do it with her bare hands. I'll get the ring for you but can I ask, why leave it in your truck?"

His brother's choice of words perplexed Ennis. What did he mean by *after what he'd seen*? When he inquired, Dane's smile withered. The older brother reverted to a quieter tone, one that read "placate" all over it, "Nothin'. I just figure the girl can handle herself. Why did you leave the ring in your truck?"

Disgruntled at the attempt to divert the subject, Ennis stated, "I was planning on proposing to her sooner rather than later. Now why did you say what you did?"

"Ennis, don't bark at me. You're startin' to sound like one of those little dogs. We've all been on edge, waiting to see about you."

"Stop stalling," was all he had the strength to say. He was weary of battling for a simple explanation. He knew all too well about Savannah's nature and stress compounded her temper. With him sidelined and unconscious, Ennis sincerely dreaded learning what happened and who it involved.

Dane squirmed. His hands slid in his pockets while a frown migrated across his features, "This is something she should tell you. Don't get me in trouble with her."

"Tell me, damn it. I won't let on you told."

12

It was loud, at least to her. The raucous noise Savannah heard repeated itself in a rhythmic manner until she felt convinced she'd lose her mind. After a moment she realized it was snoring. Since they'd been together, Ennis possessed a snore that could, with little encouragement, wake the dead. With slight fine tuning, universes light years away would hear him. And when she tried to sleep, it positively ripped her.

Ennis drifted back to sleep once talking with his brother so the room fell still and quiet, an invitation too good to pass up. She'd nodded off after Dane and Georgia left on a mystery journey, Georgia looking giddy and Dane resembling a deer in the headlights. Whatever they planned, Savannah hoped it lasted a while because exhaustion finally overwhelmed her. She never felt so drained in her life. For the first time in a week, Savannah welcomed sleep and for the first time, only dreams danced in her weary mind. Until the snoring began...

A touch on her arm startled her awake, her eyes blinking to clear away the blurriness. She surveyed the room to find no one there. Once she turned in Ennis's direction, she saw his eyes open and a tired smile on his face as he lightly brushed her arm again, "Mornin', Sleeping Beauty."

"Mornin'," she yawned. "Did you get some rest?"

She sensed him restraining a laugh, "Yeah, till someone started snoring and woke me up."

Now Savannah sported the same look Dane had when he left, "That was *me*?"

He chuckled now, "'Fraid so." Another coughing spasm raked through him, bringing Savannah to her feet with concern. He waved her back down, "Dane said you hadn't slept since this happened."

"Not much, no. I couldn't rest until you were okay. I'm sorry I woke you."

"You're fine. It's not like I haven't had enough sleep."

She noticed he stared at her until she seated herself again. They'd known each other long enough to realize when something bothered the other. Judging by his eyes, something perturbed him. Plus, when Ennis Rutherford clammed up, he was troubled. "What's wrong, Ennis?"

He blinked slowly as if trying to phrase his response politically. It seemed he settled on, "How's work?"

Savannah's blue eyes lowered. In her life she found it particularly easy to lie to most people. Maybe it was the job, maybe it was just her. There were two people she could never snow over – Georgia and Ennis. Problem was, she really didn't *want* to snow Ennis about anything. She only hedged to protect him until his strength returned, until he came home. "I'm no use there right now. Once you're home, maybe it'll be different."

"Savannah," his voice lilted like he knew a secret. "Tell me."

"Tell you what?" Her tone hardened slightly, a defense acquired since childhood. When cornered on a subject, her personality switched from friendly to protective. Since she'd known Ennis, her temper toned down considerably but even he incurred her wrath when he pushed too hard.

He laid his hand atop hers and squeezed gently, "If we're gettin' hitched, I think trust is one of those vital criteria. You know, like love, faithfulness, and you obeying my every command."

The conclusion to his statement brought her vision back to his, an eyebrow arched with incredulity and humor, "You can expect to see a lot more of this place if you expect that *obeying every command* part."

Ennis chuckled which brought a smile from her. His thumb stroked the back of her hand, "There's something you're not telling me about work. What is it?"

Savannah took his hand and kissed it. Her lips lingered while she gave serious thought about telling him. A few moments passed, "It's nothing that can't wait until you're better. That's all I care about."

His brow sank forcing her to ward off any lecture, "Ennis, seriously. It's not about trust, it's about you coming home." She closed her eyes, grateful he was alive to argue with. For days she'd weighed the importance of their jobs against the importance of their happiness together. She decided to broach the subject at a later date. She really wanted Ennis to find a safer job. Of course he'd say the same of her then they'd hit an impasse. That was, if she still *had* a job. Her instinct leaned toward purchasing farmland and a few chickens as a precautionary measure.

"Don't leave me in the dark long, sugar."

"I'll tell you soon."

13

Morning sunlight brightened Ennis's room, casting a warm, golden hue across his bed and along the polished floor. Ennis loved mornings. Savannah figured it went back to growing up on a ranch in the wide open expanse of the Texas Panhandle. "You haven't lived until you've seen a sunrise or sunset there," he'd said times before. He spoke of his home with utmost pride and just a hint of melancholy. Savannah knew he missed Texas. No matter how beautiful Atlanta was, he'd always miss home.

She stroked his hand, noticing a few little scars on the back, palm and wrist. Probably the result of working on the ranch, she thought. That or the mischievousness of boys playing rough like boys often did. She held his hand in hers and softly drew her other down his long, meaty fingers. Ennis's hands were large, strong. She always felt safe in his embrace.

Voices in the hallway pulled her attention from him

momentarily. While he slept, the hospital never totally quieted down. People padded along the halls at all hours, the PA system remained active through the night. For the most part, the room maintained a generous degree of peace. Ennis awoke only twice, both times calling her name. When he heard her respond, he relaxed returning to sleep once again.

Looking at her watch, she guessed he was close to waking up. Since he emerged from the coma, she looked forward more and more to her moments with Ennis. Whether a long conversation or a simple squeeze on her hand, she cherished them all.

A whispering sound caught her attention. She turned to see Josh and barely stifled the groan struggling for freedom. His expression was one to dread. She'd hoped for a private conference when this day came, not a meeting in front of Ennis who'd probably wake up any second.

Internal Affairs barely let the ink dry on her separation papers before sending her captain to officially notify her. The jerks could have waited another day just for looks.

She noticed how impeccably Josh dressed for a slaughter. His muscular form fit perfectly in the blue suit, his badge clipped to his belt. She considered Josh Hunter attractive in most ways. For his age, he sported few gray hairs in the thick mass of brown and little lines creased his brow. He didn't smile much but being a police captain didn't promote warm, fuzzy feelings most times. She thought about that a moment and decided being on her end of the stick didn't promote too many smiles either.

Instead of entering, Josh leaned in the room to whisper, "Do you *ever* check your voice mail?"

She nodded toward Ennis, whispering in response, "I've been slightly busy."

He waved her out, "I need to talk to you –"

"Hey, boss," a lethargic, gravelly voice interrupted, prompting Savannah to hold back another groan. Ennis, as she feared, awoke at precisely the wrong time. She refused to be dismissed from the job while in his presence. The punishment would be received in a quiet, remote place where she could take time to accept the consequences and wind down to a calmer level *then* she'd tell Ennis...

A tense smile crossed Josh's lips, "Hi, Ennis. How're you getting along?"

"I'll be back to work in no time," he smiled at Savannah. "Back with my partner and solving crime."

Josh shifted his vision away, and awkwardness settled in Savannah's gut. No doubt it settled in her expression as well.

Ennis sensed the chill in the room, "Okay, what's going on? And don't say 'nothing' and don't say you'll tell me later." He launched into a coughing spasm that, as always, sent her straight to his side to help if possible. His arm cradled his chest and he winced with pain. Once he calmed down, Ennis wrapped his hand around hers, "Tell me right now."

"Ennis," Josh resumed visual contact, "it's really between me and Savannah. She can tell you after we finish."

He tightened his hold, his tone increasingly more insistent, "Savannah." With one word Ennis made his point. No more stalling. He didn't want answers, he commanded them. Over time his physical strength returned and his grasp accentuated his tone.

Savannah finally sighed, "I'll tell you when we're done." She tugged at her hand but Ennis clasped it firmly. She got the message loud and clear, "I promise."

"You'd better," he replied. "I'm tired of being a mushroom."

Even with the anxiousness coursing through her gut, she managed a sweet kiss to his pursed lips, "I'll be back." If anyone felt like a mushroom, it was her. Tons of excrement had been heaped on her daily, leaving her to struggle her way to fresh air.

She gathered the remnants of her nerves and followed Josh out of the room. They walked in silence – which boded unfavorably in her opinion – until they stood outside the hospital, a fair distance from any foot traffic or prying ears.

The sun warmed her shoulders, the breeze felt practically insignificant causing the usual Atlanta humidity to sink to her bones. Between that and her nerves, a fine sheen of sweat began surfacing on her forehead and face. By Josh's features, he labored to prepare a long-dreaded speech. Savannah braced herself while trying to appear calm. She watched traffic funnel off a side street into the parking lot. The cars traveled past them, their drivers oblivious to her inner turmoil. *This is it*, she thought. *The culmination of my career.* All the years of hard work, the gold shield she worked so hard for, and worst of all, her reputation were all history. The worst of it being Patrick Dockery would probably roam the city streets, raping women to his heart's content because of her actions. The pain and suffering Ennis currently endured was all for nothing because she took the law into her own hands and lost.

Josh did nothing to alleviate her worries, "I can't understand you. All the hell you've taken from other cops, the brass. To piss it all away like that…"

"Okay," she interjected to hush his lecture. "Rake me

over the coals later. I can't even express how regretful I am for putting you and my colleagues in that position. But," she took a long breath, "I don't regret trying to kill that asshole."

Josh waved his hands as a sign to shut up, "Savannah, don't dig yourself deeper." He shoved a hand through his thick hair, "God sakes, that's what got you into this position. Not thinking."

"Am I off the job? Just tell me, *please*," she begged. The anticipation engulfed her, weakened her to the point she propped against the brick wall, welcoming the stability. Funny how nerves made a person shaky, she thought. Her hands and legs quivered like she stood naked in a snowstorm. She bit her bottom lip, nibbling it between her teeth. She'd kicked that habit years ago - like she had drinking - but knew if she got fired she'd be fighting both demons all over again.

Josh frowned at her, "You'll hear me out first and stop biting your lip. You look like a damn kid." He looked down at her, letting his height speak for itself, "I can't have my detectives turning vigilante on me. It gives me, my station and my officers a bad name. FYI, if you and Ennis are involved, keep it to yourselves or I'll transfer one of you." He took a brief breather, calmed down slightly, and continued, "After IA interviewed his training officer, Connelly confessed to lying about seeing you go in with Dockery. Guess he just wanted a little spotlight of his own. I don't know what my people are doing anymore. In case you're wondering, that's not a good thing. I've got you running around waving guns and trying to kill suspects while another is lying out his ass and all the others catch a sudden case of amnesia."

The latter part of the statement confused her, "Amnesia? What do you mean?"

He threw his hands skyward as if asking for guidance, "Ask any one of them what they saw that day, you know what they say? 'Nothing. I saw nothing.' The most they admit to is you confronting Dockery – without a weapon. Don't you find that odd? Correct me if I'm wrong but that *was* a gun we pried from your hand, right?" Now he leveled his gaze on her, "Do you know how deep the shit will be if Internal Affairs finds proof of what really happened?"

"Then you'll get that vacation you've been wanting."

His brow sank further, "Yeah, an unpaid one because I followed my lemmings over the cliff and said there was a verbal confrontation between you and Dockery but nothing I couldn't handle. I failed to mention the gun or the fact it took me, half my squad, and yours and Ennis's brothers to pull your stubborn ass off the guy."

The declaration caught her up short. Josh Hunter protected his detectives and cops except when they royally screwed up. She considered her stunt the crown jewel by now. For him to back up everyone's stories floored her. Now she understood why John Mathis instructed her as he had. He, along with her colleagues, designed the whole story. She stammered for words but couldn't drag one out to save her life.

Josh found her struggle faintly amusing, "Good. Stay that way for another two minutes. The bottom line is you keep your shield and your partner when he returns to work. But since we all covered your ass with IA, you will do what I say. Number one, you will control that damn temper. Number two, I will dismiss you myself if you do something that stupid again. Number three, keep yours and Ennis's private life private. If your relationship interferes with your work, one of you is transferred. Number four, you will take two weeks off without pay because I personally think you need a good slap on the ass for your actions. Am I clear?"

Savannah forced an affirmative answer from her paralyzed lips, "Yes, and thank you for –"

"Okay, *here's* where you shut up because I lost a lot of sleep over that decision. Thanking me is not a good idea. Professionally, I should have your badge. Personally, I wanted to hold that son of a bitch down while we all took turns on him with tasers. I'm not heartless but I have a lot of cops to look after." He leaned down until they were eye to eye, "I cannot have a rogue detective on my watch, Savannah. I *won't* have one. Straighten up."

o o o

Ennis waited impatiently. He hoped Savannah came clean about her actions at the station. When Dane told him she'd tried to shoot his attacker, a sickness flooded him that he'd rarely experienced before. The whole station saw her or heard her. She'd be lucky to only lose her job. She'd probably face a lawsuit from the suspect. The mere thought weakened him all over again.

Everyone magically appeared after Josh and Savannah left the room. His mother, Georgia, Dane, Seth and his family all crowded his room when all he truly desired was five minutes alone with his partner to wring – or guilt – the truth from her.

On a brighter note, Dane brought the engagement ring with him which buoyed his mood temporarily. He hadn't expected to propose in front of a crowd but choices seemed limited when it came to his life lately.

He secreted the ring box beneath the blanket. Depending on Savannah's expression and mood, he'd decide when to spring his formal proposal.

Georgia leaned closer, whispering, "It's a beautiful ring, Ennis. I stole a peek at it on the way here."

"Think she'll like it?" he asked.

Her features eased into a smile reminding him of Rita Hayworth's Gilda. Georgia nodded, patted his shoulder, "She'll fall in love with you all over again."

While his mother walked in, Ennis noticed a few items in her possession. She carried a can of Dr. Pepper, a bottle of aspirin, a Louis L'Amour book (he assumed was for him) and bridal magazines he assumed were intended for Savannah. He shooed the magazines aside but it soon became clear his mother had a mission. The engagement announcement had been made – albeit informally – but she insisted that early preparations were vital. Mama opened a magazine to a particular page, its upper corner creased for a bookmark, "She'd look absolutely darlin' in this dress, don't you think?"

One look at the wedding gown and Ennis's heart rate doubled. Savannah wouldn't look darlin', she'd look irresistible. She'd be the sexiest bride in history. It didn't help since the magazine model resembled his sweetheart in some ways with her dark, wavy hair and dazzling blue eyes. The white strapless, multi-tiered lacy dress clung to the model's curves until flaring out at the bottom. The thought of Savannah wearing it made his soul ache.

Ennis grimaced in an attempt to gain control of his thoughts and body's reaction. Images like that were meant for healthy, un-hospitalized men and he still climbed toward that goal. "Ma, she would look beautiful but this isn't a subject we should be deciding for her." *But I'll certainly have a talk with her about this particular dress...*

"Never hurts to be prepared," she assured. "I marked the ones I really like, to give her a few ideas."

He felt his brow drawing downward. Evidently the wedding took on a life of its own while he and Savannah weren't looking. Next he figured his sister-in-law might choose the colors of the ceremony, instead of Savannah as was customary. Then Ennis remembered – nothing was customary about his family or hers.

Mama considered his expression, "Don't frown, Ennis. They're only suggestions. Savannah's open-minded enough to listen to suggestions."

That's what *she* thought... His mother had yet to

experience the true molten rage bubbling beneath Savannah's surface. Losing control of anything pissed her off. Losing control of her wedding tended to piss off any normal woman so he trembled to think how Savannah would react, "We don't even know if we're having a big wedding. She may not want one." Ennis wished he hadn't said that. The stunned looks from every warm body in the room told him a small wedding was simply out of the question.

"You're kiddin', right?" Dane inquired after working his tongue loose. "Doesn't every woman want a big wedding?"

"Not every woman," Georgia answered quietly which perked Dane's ears and towed Ennis's attention to his brother. He possessed the look Ennis sported for the better part of a year and a half – a lovesick one. Wishing his strength didn't ebb so quickly, he gave Dane a cautious frown instead of a private lecture. Georgia still tried to gather the remains of her life after her divorce, she didn't need his brother hanging on her 24/7. Strangely, Georgia hadn't shied from Dane's touch or nearness. In fact, she appeared to nestle against him as his arm curled around her waist.

Ennis shook his head, wondering if he'd been out longer than he thought. Since when did those two get so cozy? After their initial meeting, Ennis expected Georgia to ban Dane

Rutherford not only from her house but her vocabulary. His brother's foot resided in his mouth more often than Ennis's – and that took genuine effort. But Georgia thought his sense of humor was "sweet" and actually described him as "adorable". Two words definitely never used in the same sentence with Dane.

Resigned to let sleeping dogs lie, he returned to the original topic, pleading, "The woman finally agreed to marry me. Let's not chase her off with talk of guest lists and registries."

Lindsey propped her elbows on the end of the bed, fascinated by the wedding talk, "Where ya gettin' married, Uncle Ennis?"

"We don't know yet, honey."

Mama offered a suggestion, "How about the ranch? There's plenty of room and it's perfect for such occasions."

Well, Ennis expected that one. He rubbed his face with his palms, trying to retain his composure, "Can I talk to Savannah about it, *please*?"

"I'd love to see Texas!" Lindsey's exuberance blossomed now. "Do you have horses and cows?"

Almost as if on cue, Mama Rutherford began describing their ranch so colorfully even Ennis wanted to go home again.

She transformed into a tourist guide about everything regarding the area, including what attire to bring for each of the four seasons. And yes, she counted off every animal residing at the ranch much like Noah when he loaded each pair of critters onto his big ol' ark.

Lindsey hung on each word until her exuberance got the best of her, "Get married in Texas, Uncle Ennis. *Please...* Talk to Aunt Savannah-"

"Talk to Aunt Savannah about what?" a female voice innocently inquired. Ennis wanted to duck under the covers as his sweetheart entered the room. She still directed her attention to Lindsey, one brow raised but the beginnings of a grin peeking through.

The little girl raced to her aunt and wrapped her arms around Savannah's waist, "Please get married in Texas. I want to see the horses and cows and chickens and ducks and -"

"Someone's campaigning awfully hard," she mentioned while returning the girl's bear hug.

Ennis jerked his thumb toward his mother, "Her fault."

Savannah kneeled down to her niece long enough to address the issue, "Sweetheart, I believe you could sell ice to an Eskimo. Let me talk to Uncle Ennis when he feels better."

Mama Rutherford adapted a coy demeanor, "Savannah,

honey, we'd love to have the wedding at the ranch but, as my son reminded, it is yours and his decision."

Ennis couldn't stifle a chuckle even as his mother reached for the bridal magazines she'd brought. He quickly grabbed them, "Oh no, you don't. That's also a decision she makes, not anyone else."

Surprisingly unflustered, Savannah placed a kiss to Ennis's lips and once more thanked God for bringing her beloved back. "So you're choosing my wedding dress too? Wow, a lot happens when I'm gone."

He slipped his hand around her forearm to prevent her from standing up. Pulling her back down, he whispered, "What's the status of your employment?" Granted, his phrasing needed refining and the narrowed vision she adapted told him so. He wasn't supposed to know until she felt comfortable explaining but waiting drained him of energy and patience. When Dane confessed to the rampage at the station and the degree of her rage, Ennis felt sick all over again. He also realized how much she loved him which aided in easing his stomach - but not by much. The images floating in his brain found him restless when he slept and edgy when awake. She refused to confess, Dane told him, until she knew Ennis was well on the road to recovery. According to Dane, though, the scene brought every cop to a precarious line. They all wanted her to kill the bastard but allowing it to happen destroyed not only her reputation but her career as well. Ennis winced when Dane described how Josh Hunter manhandled her and slammed her against the wall. He certainly never doubted the degree of her temper once it flared. He'd never seen her completely uncontrollable but he understood it. If their roles were reversed, their colleagues would have to drag Ennis off the bastard too.

He cupped Savannah's cheek and kissed her, hoping to diffuse her anger, "Don't be upset. I just want to know about your job." When she remained silent a moment, he debated over the reason. Was it because she was dismissed from the job or was it because someone tattled to him? He retraced the past few minutes, remembering how cavalier she acted about the wedding plans. It wasn't the job she stewed over so hopefully she still retained that. It was the tattling she fumed about. Her mind began seeking the culprit, flipping through possibilities. Ennis knew her and he knew precisely when her mind tripped onto "Seth" and "Dane". He did his best to divert her attention, "Stop stalling and tell me."

"We're still partners both off and on the job. If we keep our personal activities hush-hush around Josh, we can stay that way."

"And I was looking forward to the toaster he'd give us as a wedding present."

The statement caught her off guard and a grin broke the annoyance. Ennis smiled in response. Sometimes he succeeded in defeating her moods with one quip. Other times it took much more. Today the happiness bubbled from her and once she chuckled, it raised everyone else's interest.

"Wait till the wedding, kids. Giggling like that only produces naughty thoughts," Dane warned good-naturedly. "And Ma is the only licensed chaperone in the group."

Seth crossed his arms in an attempt to look fatherly, "I bet I could manage. I've got a couple of kids, you know."

Georgia put her two cents in, "Just try and keep these two away from each other. There'll be a killin' if you do."

"Look who's talking," Savannah mumbled as she rose straight again. Ennis nodded with his own raised brow.

He reached beneath the covers for the ring box.

Seth bent down, whispering to his daughter, "He's about to ask her."

Excitement overwhelmed Lindsey who nudged her way in front of her aunt, "I want to see, I want to see."

Puzzled at the actions and outburst, Savannah glanced

around for an answer. Seth sighed and lifted his hands to his face, "Sorry, sis. Lindsey's front and center for all occasions, as you know."

"What occasion?" she asked, still in the dark.

Lindsey took her aunt's right hand and brought it closer to Ennis, waiting.

Georgia smiled, "Other hand, sweetie."

The little girl immediately switched hands, taking Savannah's left and holding it for Ennis. Realization finally dawned on Savannah who held her niece closer while Ennis opened the ring box. His hands shook as bad as Savannah's now, only she had Lindsey to support hers and conceal the trembling. He took a deep breath, hoping the ring fit as well as he'd planned. The silver band with three diamonds mounted across the top cost a reasonable amount of money but he wanted the best (for what he could afford) for Savannah.

He chanced a glimpse at her face. Tears gathered even as Lindsey begged him to hurry. Ennis hated to tell the girl. He'd waited so long for Savannah, he wanted to take his time and do it right. Situating the ring for slipping it on her finger was tricky at first. His large fingers refused to grip it correctly and when they did, he feared bending the ring in half from nerves. "You ready?" he asked.

She nodded, blinked away the growing tears. With that nod, he realized she feared breaking down in front of everyone. Of course he was rather nervous himself. His shaking hand took her left one while his other managed to slip the ring on effortlessly. Ennis breathed a sigh of relief. Then he spoke the words he'd dreamed of for so long, "Savannah, will you marry me?"

Holding back the emotion became futile for her. Even while sweeping away tears that rolled down her cheeks, she nodded, "I will marry you, anytime, anywhere."

Lindsey tilted her head back to see her aunt smiling and weeping, "You're not s'pposed to cry, Aunt Savannah. You're s'pposed to be happy."

Savannah held on to Ennis's hand, holding it, "Honey, I couldn't be any happier."

14

Patrick Dockery never stood a chance. His efforts to have charges dropped because of police brutality failed but the one bright moment of his miserable life came when he made bail. A short thirty-four hours into his newfound freedom, he found himself staring down the loaded weapon of yet another angry woman. This time his luck ran out. He broke into an upscale Atlanta home with lofty expectations of having a good time with the female living there. He climbed the stairs and located his intended victim sleeping soundly in her bed. His plans changed when the woman sat up, armed with a .45 she'd retrieved from beneath a nearby pillow.

According to the victim, upon sight of the weapon, he uttered the words "not again" just before she shot him. Had Patrick Dockery surveyed his surroundings before entering the bedroom, he'd have noticed the gun case in the upstairs hallway stocked with rifles and various handguns. If he'd done his homework, he'd have noticed the certificates hanging along that wall stating Abigail Griffith was a member in good standing with the NRA and had been for twenty years.

Upon hearing the news of Dockery's death, neither Savannah or Ennis shed a tear. Instead, they busied themselves with wedding plans. They took time out to exchange their belated anniversary gifts. Ennis presented the mystery Tiffany's gift shortly after his release from the hospital. He also asked that she consider wearing it on their wedding day. Before opening the gift, she agreed to. Based on the engagement ring, his taste in jewelry (and most things in general) was magnificent. When she lifted the top off the box, the heart shaped pendant inlaid with small diamonds literally stole her breath. It took every ounce of self control not to leap with joy into Ennis's arms. Instead she thanked him with a kiss then presented her belated anniversary gift to him, praying it delighted him as much as the pendant thrilled her. The watch she'd bought brightened his face like a kid's on Christmas morning. He studied it front and back until he laid eyes on the engraving. "To My One and Only. Love Forever, Savannah."

When she and Ennis planned the wedding, she realized there was one snag that could never be overcome. Her father insisted he give her away. She expected it since he'd given Georgia away at her wedding. She remembered the joy of *that* occasion, chasing R.J. away from the liquor to ensure he walked Georgia down the aisle and not vise versa.

After mentally reliving that gem, Savannah politely refused R.J., explaining she'd already chosen a candidate for the job. A much more worthy candidate, in her opinion. R.J. threw a predictable drunken conniption so she frosted it by announcing the wedding was in Texas which, at that point, hadn't been confirmed. Attempting to regain the upper hand, R.J. refused to attend. Savannah just shrugged. His decision suited her fine. What didn't suit her was the tongue-lashing he laid on her as she left the house. She'd driven off with him still hollering expletives out the front door at her. That's when she called the man she *really* wanted to stand in for R.J. – Seth agreed without a moment's hesitation.

She and Ennis elected to have the wedding at the Rutherford Ranch, as Lindsey so energetically requested. Savannah decided it best for a few reasons. One, it gave her family an opportunity to acquaint themselves with Ennis's. Two, it limited the chance her father would attend and embarrass her with his drinking and boisterous, most times intolerable, personality. And three, the ranch represented a turning point in hers and Ennis's relationship many months earlier when they made a commitment to each other – in a blizzard, no less.

The families spent weeks tidying up the place and preparing it for the ceremony. Behind the house were hundreds of acres that they cordoned off into a smaller, manageable area for guest chairs and a flower covered arbor for the couple.

The day of the ceremony Georgia spent the better part of two hours fussing over Savannah's hair and dress, the latter being similar to a dress Ennis found in a magazine. The only exception was the lavender sash instead of the periwinkle in the photo.

Every single bridesmaid argued over her hair. They preferred Savannah's hair up which completely contradicted her plans. She diplomatically explained that Ennis preferred her hair down and that's the way it would be. The subject required no further discussion.

Georgia, Seth's wife Leah and Ennis's sister-in-law Bobbi served as bridesmaids and all wore beautiful lavender dresses that Mama Rutherford said complimented the bride very well. Anxiety rooted deep when Lindsey, the flower girl, began the trek down the aisle, sprinkling rose petals so precisely Savannah worried she might be obsessive compulsive.

She watched nervously as the little girl proceeded down the aisle a little too fast for her taste. Savannah knew her cue loomed close. She glanced out the door long enough to see the groom's side was, for obvious reasons, filled to capacity. The bride's side of the aisle was far less crowded with relatives from the Prince and Culberson families. Also sitting with them were some of their closest colleagues from work, including John Mathis. In short, just enough people to make a nice wedding and also enough to give the bride an ulcer. What if she tripped? Worse, what if Seth couldn't catch her in time? She'd roll down the aisle to Ennis, not walk. Oh, why did she agree to this wedding? Why didn't she insist on a small, private ceremony where walking wasn't necessary? Standing was a challenge in itself.

At the first notes of the "Wedding March", nerves hijacked any reserve calm she may have stowed away between her "something borrowed" and "something blue". Unfortunately Seth made it worse when he said, "Let's get you married, sis."

Yes, let's, she told herself, *and the quicker the better because I'm fast losing the feeling in my legs.* She settled for nodding to her brother. It seemed safer than trying to speak, especially since she felt dizzy and a little sick. It figured, she thought. Her body chose to mutiny on the very day she couldn't afford it. The happiest day of her life and she was going to toss her cookies, she just knew it.

Seth covered her hand with his, "Settle down. It's just you and Ennis now."

Yeah, sure, she thought. *And fifty onlookers...* She smiled as all brides do while proceeding toward the alter but even Seth felt the tension in her. He leaned closer whispering, "Stop worrying and focus on Ennis." She did, and in that instant, her stomach settled and her smile relaxed.

Dressed in his tuxedo, Ennis looked like a movie star. He stood straight and proud, his grin beaming from ear to ear. Her sweetheart waited patiently as she made her way to him. Savannah expressed another thanks to God for bringing her sweetheart back to her.

Ennis winked at her and a rush of heat warmed her cheeks. Yes, God deserved plenty of credit in her book. He made her dream come true.

She momentarily turned her vision to Georgia who wore a generous smile of her own. Savannah didn't mind admitting her sister had been right several months earlier. She'd predicted a marriage. At the time, Savannah rewarded her with an expression indicating Georgia must have suffered a mental break. Savannah and marriage? Never. She soon learned – never say never...

She and Seth finally made it to the alter and her brother took his place beside Jake as one of Ennis's groomsmen. Dane stood as best man followed by Cal, Jake and Seth. Monty, Cal's young son, took his responsibility as ring bearer as seriously as Lindsey took hers as flower girl. He guarded the rings with the vehemence of a bulldog. At his appointed time, he stood front and center, presenting the rings as rehearsed.

The vows were intentionally brief. Neither Savannah or Ennis felt they could survive writing their own vows, much less speak them in modern day English. Their tongues would be lucky to speak the "I Do's" without seizing up so they settled for a brief exchanging of vows. As Dane said, "We all know you're nuts over each other. Just say the words, smooch and get on with the festivities."

Savannah assumed nothing could ruin the wedding after they'd completed the customary vows. The weather held to near ideal conditions, everyone looked idyllic for the day and her father stayed in Augusta, probably drowning his sorrows in scotch. Yes, Savannah assumed the day was ending as storybook perfect as she and Ennis hoped. She assumed wrong. The preacher approached the famous line about anyone objecting to the couple's union and she heard a female clearing her throat.   There was no mistaking that voice.   Ennis recognized it too. Savannah glanced past Ennis to Jake who threw the nastiest glare into the crowd she'd ever seen from a Rutherford boy. With one withering glower, Jake managed to silence Jenny Lee Crawford, a major feat in itself.

The preacher, sensing the tension mounting, quickly pronounced them "husband and wife" and Ennis barely waited for the "kiss the bride" prompt. He drew her to him by the waist and the kiss he laid on her melted her bones, made her dizzy and deliriously happy all at the same time. The intensity of Ennis's kiss forced her to cling to his shoulders for stability. The world spun as they shared their first kiss as husband and wife.

They parted from the kiss, and Ennis smiled down at her, "It's nice to finally meet you, *Mrs. Rutherford.*"

Savannah stood to tiptoe and kissed him again. It was good to finally *be* Mrs. Rutherford. They agreed beforehand she'd keep her maiden name at work but otherwise, she was, without a doubt, Mrs. Ennis Rutherford, the wife of a truly magnificent man. *You were right, Mama,* she thought. *With God, all things are possible…*

J.L. Lemon lives in Texas surrounded by a loving and supportive family, two adorable and devoted puppies, and hordes of garden gnomes.

Before 2002, J.L. Lemon wrote opinions and product reviews for an online consumer guide. When fellow reviewers cited the author's knack for humor, she decided to return to writing fiction. Along with the standalone title Second Chances, she's published 9 books in the Savannah Stories Series.

Savannah and Ennis keep the author busy taking dictation and making plenty of suggestions about their future.